'You have gone
me for a favou
said, 'and such
not go unrewarded.'

'Is that a yes?' Veronica enquired hopefully.

'A qualified yes. My top hat and brand-new morning suit are at your disposal this afternoon…'

Her smile was tinged with uncertainty. 'But—?' she added, after a small pause.

'But,' he confirmed, 'I shall require a small favour… All I ask in return for my company this afternoon is that you don your wedding hat again and come to my sister's wedding as my guest.' He could see that she was puzzled. 'We'll form our own escort agency, you and I. A very exclusive one. I will keep at bay the suitors your mother has lined up for you; your task will be to fend off a gaggle of hopeful spinsters, widows and divorcees that my sisters have targeted as prospective wives for me.'

'You're joking!' she gasped.

'I sincerely wish I was,' he replied.

Born and raised in Berkshire, **Liz Fielding** started writing at the age of twelve when she won a hymn-writing competition at her convent school. After a gap of more years than she is prepared to admit to, during which she worked as a secretary in Africa and the Middle East, got married and had two children, she was finally able to realise her ambition and turn to full-time writing in 1992.

She now lives with her husband, John, in West Wales, surrounded by mystical countryside and romantic, crumbling castles, content to leave the travelling to her grown-up children and keeping in touch with the rest of the world via the Internet.

You can visit Liz Fielding's web-site via Harlequin at: http://www.romance.net

Recent titles by the same author:

GENTLEMEN PREFER...BRUNETTES
HIS LITTLE GIRL

A SUITABLE GROOM

BY

LIZ FIELDING

MILLS & BOON®

All the characters in this book have no existence outside the imagination of the author, and have no relation whatsoever to anyone bearing the same name or names. They are not even distantly inspired by any individual known or unknown to the author, and all the incidents are pure invention.

First published in Great Britain 1998
Harlequin Mills & Boon Limited,
Eton House, 18-24 Paradise Road, Richmond, Surrey TW9 1SR

ISBN 0 263 81443 2

Set in Times Roman 11 on 12 pt.
02-9901-46826 C1

Printed and bound in Norway
by AIT Trondheim AS, Trondheim

CHAPTER ONE

'THANKS for the lift, Nick.'

'It's the least I can do, considering you turned up at six this morning to go over those figures with me.' Nick Jefferson lifted Veronica's small suitcase from the boot. 'Call me when you know which train you're catching back tomorrow and I'll pick you up. In fact, why don't you come to supper? Cassie's working on a new recipe; I know she'd welcome a totally unbiased opinion, and you haven't been near her in weeks.'

'Your wife should be putting her feet up with the baby so near,' Veronica replied quickly. 'Not slaving over a hot stove for any Tom, Dick or Jane you invite home.'

'Come to supper and you can tell her yourself to take it easy, along with your opinion on her recipe,' he informed her. 'Maybe she'll listen to you.'

'I doubt it.' Veronica relieved him of her case. 'Besides, there's more than one way to keep a lady in bed, Nick. Offer to rub her back...or something.'

He grinned. 'Now why didn't I think of that? Hey, don't forget your hatbox.' She pulled a face. 'Anyone would think you don't want to go to this wedding.'

'I don't much,' she said. 'I love my cousin dearly, but family weddings are fairly close to the bottom of my list of favourite events. One above going to the dentist. Maybe. My dentist makes me laugh.'

'Then why go? It's not compulsory, is it?'

Veronica offered Nick a wry smile. 'My family take weddings seriously; you're expected to turn up unless you've got a doctor's note confirming the plague.' She regarded the hatbox with dislike. 'You don't happen to *know* a bribable doctor, do you?'

'I'm afraid not. Would a note from the boss do? ''Veronica can't come out to play until she's finished a report on the marketing of our latest line in camp fridges to Eskimos—'''

She laughed. 'Heaven forbid. I get enough grief from my mother about putting my career first as it is.' She took the cumbersome hatbox from him. 'I'd better go. Missing the train would not be an acceptable excuse either.'

Fortunately, the eight-fifteen had a dining car—the six o'clock start had left her feeling hollow, and it was going to be a long day. The steward smiled as he spotted her. 'Morning, Miss Grant. Here, let me take your bag.'

'Thank you, Peter,' she said, surrendering her small suitcase and dropping her hatbox onto the vacant chair at the two-seater table before settling herself in the opposite seat, glancing out at the platform in that still moment of expectancy while the guard glanced along the length of the train to make sure all was clear. Then, as the man raised his whistle to his lips, his attention, and hers, was caught by the brisk, sharp sound of leather-shod feet pounding up the stone steps.

'Hold that door!'

The latecomer had called out with the confident ring of someone used to instant obedience. He got it, and Veronica found herself holding her breath as a tall, lithe figure sprinted across the platform and boarded the train. The door banged shut, the whistle blew, the train slid seamlessly from the station.

'Ready to order, miss?'

She turned to the steward. 'Do my eyes deceive me, or was that Fergus Kavanagh, Peter?' she asked, surprised. She would have bet any amount of money that the Chairman of Kavanagh Industries was a chauffeur-driven Rolls man.

'Yes, miss. Travels with us most mornings. As he says, if he doesn't travel with us, who will?' He grinned at her raised eyebrows. 'He does own a sizeable chunk of this line. Do you know him?'

'No,' she said. 'Not yet.'

Fergus Kavanagh was normally the most even-tempered of men, although he would have been the first to admit that he couldn't take any great credit for that. It was simply that very few people went out of their way to irritate him.

Today, however, was not normal.

Today he would have positively welcomed the opportunity to strangle two of the most interfering, the most infuriating women it was his misfortune to be related to.

The guard, his whistle to his lips, held the door for him as he raced up the stairs to catch the eight-fifteen train into London. 'You've cut it a bit fine this morning, Mr Kavanagh.'

'I seem to be cutting my entire life a bit fine at the moment, Michael,' Fergus replied, without any noticeable lack of breath, as he stepped aboard.

The other man grinned. 'It's always the same with weddings. I've seen two daughters through it; I know what it's like. Just you concentrate on how peaceful it'll be when it's all over, and you'll sail through it.' And with those words of comfort the man blew his whistle and slammed the door.

Peace. As Fergus made his way through the crowded carriages in the direction of the restaurant car the word flickered tantalisingly, like a beacon just out of reach. Peace was a concept that had always seemed just to elude him, but he had believed, he had really believed, that after Dora's wedding it might at long last be attainable.

With both his sisters married, and now the responsibility of their respective husbands, he could concentrate on business, his estate and the simple pleasures available to a bachelor of means. He was a collector. He collected fine art, fast racehorses and profitable companies.

He should have known better. Even up to their eyes in such desperately important last-minute decisions as colour schemes for flowers and balloons, the problem of how they were going to seat three women who had all, at one time or another, been married to the same man, and where in the world they were going to find a small boy who would not object to wearing satin knee breeches, Poppy and Dora, his two darling sisters, had still found time to plot yet more mayhem with which to plague him.

Well, they could plot without him. He refused to take any further part in the proceedings. His club might be dull, but women were excluded from any part of it, and with Dora in temporary possession of his house he was quite prepared to stay there until the wedding. He would have stayed there until *after* the wedding, until every vestige of confetti had been plucked from the borders, every trace of heel-marks removed from his immaculate lawns by a bad-tempered gardener. Unfortunately, it was his duty to give away the bride and, since duty was something he had never shirked, that small personal revolution was denied him.

He paused at the entrance to the dining car and caught the steward's eye.

'Good morning, Mr Kavanagh. We're a bit full this morning. The ladies seem to be taking advantage of the special discounted fare to visit the spring sales. We don't usually see you on Friday,' he said, glancing around, 'or I'd have kept you a table. I'm afraid you'll have to share...'

Yet more irritation. He was not in the mood for company. He had been looking forward to a quiet journey, during which he could read the City pages and forget all about his sister and her wedding.

Instead, he found himself being shepherded towards a two-seater table where a woman was perusing the menu.

No, that really was the last straw. The barrier of a newspaper was enough to deter most men from fatuous conversation; women, he knew from experience, were trickier. Bringing up two younger sisters had taught him just how tricky they could be. Peter should really know better than that. But one glance was sufficient to reassure him; the seat opposite her was occupied by a large hatbox. Excuse enough to move on.

He spotted an empty space at the far end of the

compartment, but as he turned to point it out to the steward the woman forestalled him.

'Do move that tiresome hatbox and sit down,' she invited, in a low, husky voice. She had lowered the menu a little, and was regarding him over the top of it so that he could see a sweep of smooth platinum-blonde hair and a pair of the most extraordinary silver-blue eyes. As he hesitated, torn between a desire to avoid company and common courtesy, the expression in those eyes suggested that she knew precisely what was going through his mind, and was sufficiently entertained by his dilemma to stir the pot a little and see how he coped. 'I don't bite,' she promised, without a trace of a smile.

Under normal circumstances he would simply have murmured something polite but distant and kept on moving. It was her eyes that kept him riveted to the spot, her eyes and her air of authority, of a belief in herself and confidence that he would do exactly as she said. Rare qualities in a woman. Rare enough to divert him from his purpose, although her beauty alone should have been enough for that.

Assured, elegant, she was old enough to be interesting, young enough to turn heads. No. That was wrong. She had the kind of bone structure that would still be turning heads when she was ninety. And she was definitely not going to the spring sales. The heavy grey silk of her skirt was too perfect a complement for her eyes to be a chance bargain, and the pearl studs in her beautifully shaped ears had the lustre that only a natural oyster could produce. A lustre that the lady herself matched to perfection.

He realised with something of a shock that she was

one of the loveliest women he had ever seen. Yet there was more than beauty; there was a touch of mischief in those eyes that made him absolutely certain that she would prove a far more entertaining companion for the journey than his newspaper. His suddenly heightened pulse-rate was evidence enough of that. The distant table and its promise of a peaceful journey quite suddenly lost its appeal. But eagerness would be a mistake.

'If you're quite sure I wouldn't disturb you? I could easily sit further along—' The train lurched obligingly just at that moment, so that he was forced to grab the back of her seat. He smiled apologetically. 'Perhaps I'd better just sit down.'

'Perhaps you had,' she agreed, her answering smile polite, nothing more. And yet there was *something*.

Intrigued, he lifted his overnight bag onto the luggage rack next to a small Vuitton suitcase that presumably was the property of the lady. Then he picked up the hatbox.

It was light, but awkward. Clearly too large for the overhead luggage rack, and there was no room for it beneath the table, although checking this out had given him the opportunity to admire a pair of long, slender legs and narrow, well-shod feet that matched the rest of the lady.

The hatbox, however, remained a challenge to his ingenuity. But not for long.

Thrust into control of a major industrial conglomerate whilst still in his twenties, Fergus Kavanagh did not lack ingenuity, and he had fine-tuned delegation to an art form. He turned and handed the box to the steward.

'Perhaps you would be good enough to find somewhere safe to stow this, Peter,' he said, then sat down, nodded briefly to his breakfast companion and flicked open his copy of the *Financial Times*. It was what that reserved creature of habit, the English businessman, would be expected to do, and every instinct was telling him that the lady would not allow him to ignore her for long.

For a moment Veronica regarded the crisply cut dark head of hair, the glimpse of broad forehead and long, rather thin fingers holding the paper—all that was visible of Mr Fergus Kavanagh behind his *Financial Times*. And she was glad of a moment's respite.

Her heart was pounding like a drum. She hadn't felt so nervous since she had negotiated her first big contract. Kavanagh's business career suggested a man prepared to take a risk, prepared to be unconventional, but on first acquaintance he seemed nerve-rackingly distant, a touch austere.

Yet there was something about the way he was holding his newspaper, a stillness that suggested he was not reading but waiting for her to make a move. Then there was that promising smile, brief though it had been, fanning laughter lines about his eyes, almost as if he knew... Maybe, beneath the disguise of that pinstriped suit and old-school tie, there beat the heart of an adventurer after all. She certainly hoped so. In fact, she was counting on it.

'Would you care to look at my menu?' she asked after a moment. 'Whilst Peter is disposing of my hat?'

Fergus smiled under cover of his newspaper. He was human enough to enjoy being proved right. The lady's looks were Grace Kelly cool, but her voice was as sexy as sin—sin leavened with laughter. He suspected that if he peered over his newspaper those silvery eyes would be laughing at him, too, perfectly aware that his initial intention had been to pass her by, delighted that she had waylaid him. But why? She didn't look like the kind of woman who picked up strangers over the breakfast table, so why did he have the feeling that he had just been caught on a hook and was about to be reeled in?

'Thank you,' he replied, gravely polite, glancing at her briefly. Definitely laughing. The deepening creases at the corners of her mouth gave him an odd little lift to his spirits, banishing the black mood in which he had boarded the train. 'But that won't be necessary,' he said, countering her move and then making one of his own. 'Peter knows what I want.'

He was offering her an opening, and he wondered what she would do with it. Start with a polite question, perhaps? *You travel on this train regularly, then?* Or maybe it would be disbelief. *You mean, you have the same breakfast every day?* Or maybe she would take his response as a rebuff and let it go. He didn't think so. The lady wanted something. Bachelors, wealthy bachelors, developed a sixth sense for such things.

She kept him waiting for a longish pause, during which Fergus found it quite impossible to concentrate on the headline in front of him. Then she said, 'The piece about your takeover bid is on page fourteen. If that is what you're looking for.'

Takeover? So, she not only knew who he was, but followed the financial pages. He was right. She was a lot more interesting than the newspaper. He lowered it for the pleasure of looking at her more directly. And she was lovely. More than lovely. There was nothing of the chocolate box beauty about her; it went deeper than that, deeper than bone structure, perfect skin, gleaming hair. There was much more to her than that—character, a mouth quick to laugh, eyes to die for. Being reeled in by this lady, he decided, would be a pleasure.

'Takeover?' he queried, taking the bait.

'Your takeover of GFM Transport. There's a photograph of you along with the article. Not a very flattering one, I have to admit.' She paused again. 'But then, newspaper photographs are always rather lifeless, don't you think?' She made the smallest, most expressive of gestures with long, slender fingers. 'I thought perhaps you were interested in what the *FT* had to say about it.' Her shoulders moved imperceptibly in a minimalist shrug. 'The takeover, that is. But maybe you're not that bothered.' Then, when he didn't immediately reply, she said, 'I'm sorry. I shouldn't have interrupted you.' *She wasn't sorry.* 'The journalist suggested that it was an "astute" move,' she added encouragingly. *Not a bit sorry.*

'Astute?' Fergus folded the newspaper and put it on the table. A woman who read the *FT* was interesting enough to break through even the legendary reserve of the British male, and he was sure she knew it, had banked on it. 'He wasn't concerned that I was tying up capital in something of a sideshow?' he asked, testing her a little to see whether she had actually read the article, or merely scanned the headline.

'Is that what your board thought?' she asked. *Some*

of them. Not that it was any of her business. But it had been the right question.

'Is that what you think?'

'It would be presumptuous of me to have any kind of opinion on the matter. I'm sure you know what you're doing. But I've interrupted you for long enough. Please do continue reading your newspaper, Mr Kavanagh.' She let the line out a little, a skilled angler playing him like a big game fish, taking care not to strike too quickly.

'Thank you,' he said, a touch drily, but he continued to regard her thoughtfully as she handed the menu card to Peter and ordered her breakfast. 'Should I know who you are?' he asked, once the steward had departed.

'Should you?' Veronica's heart was still beating too fast. *Lord, but he was perfect. Exactly the man for the job.* He didn't immediately answer her, taking his turn to keep her waiting. She smiled as she acknowledged his silence... This was a game and she sensed that he knew it. *But would he be prepared to play?* 'There's no reason why you should, Mr Kavanagh. My name is Veronica Grant. I'm Marketing Director for Jefferson Sports.' And she offered him her hand.

Slim, fine-boned, ringless, her nails polished to a deep plum-coloured perfection—a perfect complement to her lovely mouth, Fergus thought, dragging his mind back from the orchard at Marlowe Court in high summer, and his boyhood raids on the sweet dark fruit that grew there.

But then, everything about her was perfection, from the curve of her platinum-blonde hair to the toes of her handmade shoes.

Jefferson Sports. They had their headquarters in the centre of Melchester, an elegant tower block with an exclusive shopping mall in the atrium. The company had grown out of all recognition since it had been formed by a family of well-known sportsmen to take commercial advantage of their name, but since Nick Jefferson had stepped into the top slot it had begun to spread its wings and take off in a big way. And this woman was part of the team. More than interesting.

'How d'you do, Miss Grant?' he said, taking her hand and shaking it solemnly.

'How d'you do, Mr Kavanagh?' she replied, with equal gravity. The steward arrived with a large tray. Two boiled eggs, brown toast and China tea for her. A pair of kippers, white toast and coffee for him. 'Please, do read your newspaper,' Veronica invited while the steward laid out the food. 'I shan't mind a bit. You probably hate conversation over breakfast. Most men seem to.'

He found himself wondering whom she shared her breakfast with. Then rather wishing he hadn't.

Besides, she shouldn't make unfounded judgements about him. He was not antisocial over breakfast. When Dora and Poppy stayed over at Marlowe Court, with or without their partners, he was more than happy to talk. Well, *usually* he was happy to talk. Not today. Today he was furious with the pair of them.

Miss Grant, however, mistook his silence for assent. 'I've disturbed the smooth start to your working day,' she continued apologetically. 'I do hope you won't be short-tempered with your secretary because of me.'

'I can assure you, Miss Grant, that the smooth running of my day was severely disturbed long before I boarded this train. And, since I'm not going to my office, my secretary is quite safe. But then, she's far too important to my well-being to be used as a verbal punchbag.' Her eyes lingered momentarily on his business suit, but she didn't enquire where he was going, or why. Instead, she began to lightly tap the shell of her egg. Fergus found her lack of curiosity profoundly irritating. Women were supposed to be terminally inquisitive, weren't they? He buttered his toast and forked up a mouthful of fish. 'Today,' he said before he could stop himself, 'I have to see my tailor.'

That wasn't entirely true. He didn't *have* to visit his tailor today. Any time next week would have done, but it had made as good an excuse as any for fleeing his own house in the middle of his sister's wedding preparations. Not that Dora had looked as if she had believed him. But then, Dora was irritated at having her plans frustrated.

'Your tailor?' Veronica Grant didn't look as if she believed it, either. 'Oh. I thought there might be some crisis with the takeover.'

His eyebrows rose. 'Are you an interested stockholder by any chance?' he demanded.

'No,' she said, not in the least intimidated by the sudden fierceness of his answer. 'Just interested.'

Her smile almost knocked him back in the seat. He would have suspected that she was flirting with him, except that people didn't flirt with total strangers on the eight-fifteen train into London. At least, not in his experience.

Maybe it was time he widened his experience. He got a charge when one of his horses won a race, but it didn't match this.

He tried a smile of his own. It wasn't at all difficult. His irritation had quickly evaporated in the company of this intriguing woman. 'To be honest, the visit to my tailor is an excuse,' he confided—since she didn't believe him, he might as well make a virtue out of owning up. 'My real reason for going up to town is to escape the mayhem of wedding preparations. I can assure you that a takeover is a piece of cake compared to the effort that seems to be involved in organising something as simple as a marriage ceremony.'

'You're getting married?' *That shook her. She covered it with another of those smiles, but she hadn't planned on that. Well, that was all right. Wedding bells didn't form any part of his plans, despite his sisters' plots.*

'Me? Heaven forbid.' *Just so that she knew he wasn't in the marriage market.* 'And in the unlikely event that I should ever be rash enough to take a plunge into that shark-infested pool, Miss Grant, I shall do it with the minimum of fuss. There will be no balloons, flowers or bridesmaids. I will not have a marquee erected on my lawn, or invite four hundred people to break my gardener's heart, trampling through his borders.'

Veronica Grant took a spoonful of egg. *Why on earth was her hand shaking? She simply wanted to borrow the man for the day, not marry him. Marriage played no part in her future plans.* 'The lady you decide to marry might have other ideas,' she pointed out, before eating it.

'Then the lady will have to make up her mind whether she wants a fancy wedding or a husband. I have two sisters, Miss Grant. One has already gone through the above performance. The second is about to do so. No man should be expected to go through it a third time.'

'They do say three's a charm.'

'Do they?' Fergus was not about to let that pass unchallenged. 'Then they—whoever they are—are talking through the back of their collective heads.'

'I see.' The lady was trying to hide a smile.

'It's not funny, Miss Grant.'

'Of course it isn't. In fact, I endorse your sentiments wholeheartedly.' But the smile didn't leave her eyes. It was irresistible. He just couldn't help smiling back. 'So you're taking refuge in your gentleman's club?'

He was *that* transparent? 'The temptation to stay there until the whole thing is over is almost overwhelming; unfortunately, I have to give away the bride. But at least it's given me an excuse to come up to town.'

Veronica Grant's smooth high forehead puckered in the smallest of frowns. Then she said, 'Oh, the tailor.'

'Apparently I need a new morning suit for the occasion.' And when Dora made up her mind about something, there was no point in fighting it. It was a thought to send a shiver of apprehension down his spine. 'I had a call yesterday to say that it's ready.'

'Oh.'

I need a new morning suit... That sounded so unbelievably pompous, he thought. No one *needed* a new morning suit. 'Actually, the one I inherited from my father fits like an old friend, and would have done perfectly well, but it's black,' he explained. 'Dora said it made me look like a funeral director.'

Somewhat unexpectedly, Veronica Grant laughed. It was a real laugh, and caused several people to turn in their direction. Then she shook her head. 'Weddings are hell, aren't they?'

'This one will be,' he said with feeling. And not just because it was turning his house and his life upside down. Then he remembered the hatbox. 'Is that the reason for the hat? Are you on your way to a wedding?'

'For my sins.' She concentrated on pouring her tea as the train raced through a cutting. 'My cousin is getting married. She's twenty-two and she hooked a viscount at the first attempt.'

'Oh.' He couldn't think of anything else to say.

She flashed him a look from beneath her lashes. 'That sounds terribly bitchy, doesn't it?' He didn't reply. He didn't see Miss Grant as the bitchy type, but it was quite possible that she'd been trying to hook a viscount too, and she was nearer thirty than twenty. 'I'm not jealous of Fliss, Mr Kavanagh. She's a lovely girl, and deserves a wonderful life with the man of her dreams...'

'But?'

She gave an expressive little shrug. 'But my mother will be. Jealous. She'll give me long, hurtful looks. She'll sigh a lot. She'll murmur about "biological clocks" ticking away and her desperate longing to hold her first grandchild before she moves on to that everlasting cocktail party in the sky.' Veronica illustrated this with small, theatrical gestures and expressions that summoned up her mother's reaction to perfection, and Fergus found himself grinning. He couldn't help himself.

'I take it that her demise is not imminent?'

'No. She's fifty-five, but refuses to admit to more than forty-nine and gets away with it every time. But that won't stop her having a...' She waved her spoon as she searched for an appropriate word. 'Do you suppose that there is a collective noun for prospective sons-in-law?'

'I've no idea. A proposal?' he suggested, after a moment's thought.

'A proposal?' She considered it, and then smiled appreciatively. 'A *proposal* of sons-in-law. I like that.' It was rather like someone switching on the lights when she smiled, Fergus decided. And not just any lights. More like one of those enormous Venetian crystal chandeliers. Or the Christmas lights in Regent Street. Or Blackpool Illuminations. Quite possibly all three. 'Well, there you have it,' she continued. 'I used to love family weddings, but these days they are something of a trial. My mother knows I won't be able to escape her "proposal" of prospective sons-in-law; she'll have them lined up for me like stallions at stud, each one vetted for financial acuity, with a family tree of oak-like proportions and the ability to put the magic word, "Lady" before my name.' She regarded him across the breakfast table. 'It's a nightmare,' she said.

CHAPTER TWO

FERGUS, if he'd ever given the matter any thought, might have concluded that most women would be glad to have all the hard work done for them. But, then again, perhaps not. Who wanted a partner that some well-meaning relative had decided was 'suitable'? He, more than anyone, had reason to be sympathetic.

'Is that important?' he asked. 'The "Lady" bit?'

'It is to her. I was once engaged to an earl; she's never forgiven me for not making it to the altar.'

'An earl?'

'An earl with an estate in Gloucestershire, a house in Eaton Square and a castle in Scotland.' She paused. 'Of course, it was only a little castle.'

'Is that why you changed your mind?' he asked. 'Because the castle was little?'

'No. I fortunately discovered in time that I wasn't countess material. I didn't want to give up my career, you see. That's the test, wouldn't you say? How much you're prepared to give up for someone.'

'I believe so. But would you have had to give it up? Your career?'

'I told you. I wasn't cut out to be a countess.'

Which didn't actually answer his question, he noted. 'You gave up the castle for your career?'

'Without hesitation,' she agreed.

Despite her cool manner, she was finding the conversation difficult. But he persevered. 'Then it's the idea of marriage that's repellent, rather than your mother's choice of suitable grooms?'

'I've no particular objection to marriage as an institution, Mr Kavanagh. I can see that the right wife to organise his domestic life must be a wonderful asset for any man.' *His sisters would undoubtedly agree with her.* 'Unfortunately, I'm far too busy organising my own life to undertake the task for anyone else. I know my own limitations and I'm just not *wife* material.' She paused. 'I just don't have the necessary qualifications.'

'I didn't know you could take a course in it. City and Guilds?' he asked. 'Or Royal Society of Arts examinations? Do they run a course for prospective husbands?'

'Maybe they should.' Her smile was a touch strained. 'I do always find myself asking, if all these thirty-something bachelors are so perfect, why hasn't someone snapped them up long ago?'

'It's an interesting question, Miss Grant,' he replied thoughtfully. 'Maybe, like the best wines, they need a little extra time to mature.'

The touch of irony was not lost on her, and for just a moment he thought he detected the faintest blush colour her cheeks. 'Oh, dear. That was tactless of me, wasn't it?'

'Probably,' he agreed easily. 'But illuminating. Tell me, is your opinion based on personal experience or simple prejudice?'

She allowed herself the smallest of smiles. 'I refuse to say another word on the grounds that I may incriminate myself.'

'That's a pity. I was rather enjoying the conversation.' And to reassure her, he went on, 'I have to admit my own pitiful excuse for not coming up to scratch is simply that I've been far too busy.'

Her brows shot up. 'Doing what?' Then there was that hint of a blush again. 'Perhaps I shouldn't ask.'

'Working, raising my sisters. I was dumped in at the deep end when my parents died a year after I graduated.'

'I'm so sorry.' And the quick compassion in her eyes told him that she wasn't simply being polite. 'My own father died when I was at university. I still miss him. So does my mother. They were, I think, the most perfectly happy couple—always together.'

'Mine too. And they died together, too. I don't think either one of them would have been capable of living without the other.' It was the kind of love that seemed to strike every member of his family sooner or later. He wasn't sure whether he welcomed the idea of it happening to him or dreaded it, and in a sudden flash of insight he wondered if maybe, after all, that was why he had so assiduously avoided all the marriage lures thrown in his path during the years. Then he realised that Veronica Grant was waiting for him to continue. 'Unfortunately my father had no interest in business, or anything very much except my mother. Kavanagh Industries was in comfortable decline, everyone too cosy to institute the painful process of bringing it up to date; the family estate was in much the same situation, and I had two considerably younger sisters to distract me should I ever find myself with five minutes to spare.' Not that he hadn't had his moments. But he'd never allowed things to progress to anything deeper, more involving. Never even been tempted.

There was a moment of awkward silence, and then Veronica said, 'Work can take over.'

'And teenage angst is not conducive to romance,' he continued with relief. 'Either Poppy or Dora always seemed to have some crisis...' And they had always come first. While he had been talking, he had been toying with his breakfast. Now he straightened and looked at her. 'Why are you still on the marriage market, Miss Grant?'

Having bared his own soul for her curiosity, he decided it was perfectly reasonable to expect her to do the same for his, and she did not appear to object. Yet she regarded him levelly for a moment, as if wondering whether he was really interested, or simply passing the time. 'I'm not *on* the marriage market, Mr Kavanagh. I told you, I'm not wife material.'

'You've never even come close since the earl?'

'Have you?' she demanded.

Fergus sat back. 'I apologise. It was impertinent of me to ask.'

She seemed to take a moment, gather herself. 'No, Mr Kavanagh, I'm sorry for snapping. You see, most people don't dare bring up the subject.' She took a bite of her toast. 'I'm considered rather formidable,' she confided. 'Except, of course, by my mother, who is formidable with a capital F. She believes that marriage is the only *suitable* occupation for a lady.'

'She's a bit old-fashioned?'

'Positively prehistoric.'

'Perhaps you should have just sent your regrets to your cousin, along with your best wishes,' he suggested. An option not open to him. 'Attendance isn't compulsory if you're not one of the major players.'

'On the contrary, in my family we expect a full turn-out for dress occasions. Weddings, christenings, special anniversaries—'

'Funerals?'

'Those too.

'And I'm very fond of Fliss. I couldn't miss her big day. Besides, if I didn't go, people would think I was sulking.'

'Because of the biological clock ticking away in your ear?'

There was a pause, brief, barely noticeable, but it was there. 'I don't think my biological clock ever got wound up,' she said.

Fergus regarded her thoughtfully. 'So why does it matter what people think?' She didn't strike him as a woman who lived in awe of either her mother or other's opinions, but she gave the smallest of sighs.

'It doesn't, to me. But to my mother...' She lifted her shoulders a fraction. 'And I do love her, even when she's being absolutely impossible.'

He could understand that. He loved Poppy and Dora, and they were impossible most of the time.

'You said it: weddings are hell.' He forked up a little of one of the kippers. 'Couldn't you take along an escort as protective colouring?' he suggested, after a moment. Dora had put 'and partner' on invitations to people whose relationships were informal or uncertain. 'There must be someone you know, work with, perhaps, you could have asked along?'

'I thought about it, but I couldn't find anyone who would do.' She glanced up. 'Women have to be so careful when they're in business. It's so easy for motives to be...misunderstood. Besides, all the nicest men I know are married.' She concentrated on her egg for a while and he, too, gave his breakfast his undivided attention. Well, almost undivided attention. Veronica Grant was not a presence it would ever be possible to totally ignore. 'I actually did consider *hiring* someone,' she said, after a while.

'Hiring someone? Are wedding guest agencies listed in the *Yellow Pages*?' If so, he might be tempted to use their services himself.

'No, but escort agencies are.' She saw his expression and shook her head. 'Not that kind of escort agency. There's one which provides well-groomed men who are guaranteed to know which fork to use and not to flirt with your best friend.'

'Is that important?'

'The fork or the flirting?' she enquired.

'Both.'

'Absolutely vital if you want to provoke envy. A friend of mine hired an escort when she had been invited to a rather grand party at which she knew her ex-husband would be appearing with his new trophy wife. She said it was worth the fee just to see his jaw drop when she waltzed in with this dishy man who was at least five years her junior. He could dance, too. The escort. A skill her ex had never been able to master. The trophy wife actually flirted with *him*.'

'A perfect result, then.'

'A-plus,' she agreed. 'And at the end of the evening it was a quick shake of the hand, a cheque in an envelope and goodnight. No strings. No complications.'

'It's an interesting idea.'

'I have to admit that I was sorely tempted. They have an Italian count on their books whom I thought might be rather fun.'

'That's a terrible idea,' he said, truly hating the thought of her hiring some dreadful gigolo type. Then, because she was looking at him rather oddly, 'Your mother doesn't sound like the kind of woman to be impressed by a fake Italian count.'

'Who said he was fake? Impoverished European aristocrats have to eat too, you know. But you're right. I'm afraid a good-looking toy boy simply wouldn't cut the mustard on this occasion. I need someone who would give the appearance of being a serious contender. Someone like you, Mr Kavanagh.' She picked up her cup, sipped her tea and then replaced her cup carefully on the saucer before looking him straight in the eye. 'Which is why I bribed Peter to put you at my table.'

Fergus Kavanagh could not remember the last time that anyone had reduced him to silence. 'You *bribed* Peter?' he managed finally.

It was time to come clean, own up, face the music. 'I'm afraid so,' Veronica admitted. 'I saw your dash for the train and I asked him if you ever came into the restaurant car for breakfast. He assured me that you never missed.'

'Did he, by God? Well, I have to say that Peter is a great disappointment to me. I had always assumed that he was thoroughly discreet. Tell me, what did it take?'

Oh, Lord, he was angry. She'd got Peter into trouble and made an utter fool of herself into the bargain. For nothing. 'I'm sorry?'

Fergus was not fooled by her apparent innocence. 'What did it take to bribe him?' he said carefully.

'Oh, I see.' She hesitated, then gave a little shrug. 'I'm not sure that I should tell you.'

After the initial shock, Fergus decided that he was rather enjoying himself. 'Force yourself,' he urged.

'A ticket for the Cup Final?' she offered.

'The Cup Final?' This woman could get tickets for a sporting event at the top of every red-blooded male's wish list? 'The *FA* Cup Final?' he asked, to be quite certain. She nodded. 'But that's only a week away. There can't be any tickets left,' he said, rather stupidly.

'I have two.' It suddenly occurred to her that he wasn't so much angry as taken by surprise. 'Had two,' she amended.

'And you thought one of them worth my presence at your breakfast table?'

She put her head to one side and regarded him for a moment. In for a penny, she thought...after all she had nothing to lose... 'Now that I've met you, Mr Kavanagh, I am of the opinion that you would have been worth both tickets.'

She didn't mince her words. Formidable indeed. And Fergus couldn't bring himself to blame Peter for accepting her offer. 'I have the feeling that I should be flattered,' he said finally.

She spread her fingers in a gesture that left it entirely up to him whether he was flattered, or merely intrigued. Just as long as he was one of them. 'It was the best I could do at short notice. I had to think quickly, you see.'

He did. And she'd certainly done that. 'Your best is very good, Miss Grant.'

But was it good enough? 'Not really. Jefferson Sports are a major sponsor. I'm expected to attend and bring a guest.'

'Peter?' His disbelief was understandable.

'Peter,' she confirmed. 'He'll have a lovely day. Lunch, a chance to meet some former players—'

'I don't doubt it,' he said, cutting her short. 'But aren't you supposed to take along one of your major customers?'

'I'd far rather take someone who really enjoys the game, someone who can tell me what exactly is happening. Peter is a keen follower of Melchester Rovers, you know. And besides, major customers can pull enough strings to get their own tickets.'

'I hope Nick Jefferson sees it that way.'

'Nick has his mind on other things at the moment. Anyway, Peter *is* a customer. He bought a set of our golf clubs a few months back. I got him a discount.' Veronica Grant smiled at him, inviting him to join in her little joke. Instead, Fergus gave her an old-fashioned look. 'You know Nick?' she asked.

'I'm afraid not.'

'The man has a highly developed sense of the ridiculous,' she assured him.

'With you as his Marketing Director, he must need it.' Then, 'Suppose I hadn't co-operated?' He indicated the seat at the far end of the carriage that had originally caught his eye. 'I might have chosen to sit over there.'

She turned and glanced at the empty seat. 'You did,' she pointed out, turning back to face him. 'But

Peter stopped you by my table and I waylaid you with my hatbox. Are *you* interested in football, Mr Kavanagh? I might be able to lay my hands on another ticket, in a good cause.'

'I have a standing invitation to the Cup Final, Miss Grant.'

'Of course. Lunch with the directors, a seat in their box. Nothing less will do for Mr Fergus Kavanagh.' He didn't deny it. 'I'm not sure what else I could offer…' she paused so briefly that he might have imagined it '…a gentleman.'

He had thought for a while that she might be having a little joke at his expense. But she wasn't. 'You're serious, aren't you?'

'In deadly earnest. You see, you fit the profile perfectly.'

He considered asking just what the 'profile' might be. Then thought better of it. 'But you don't know anything about me.'

'That's not entirely true. I know, for instance, that you are the most eligible of men—that is, you're wealthy and unmarried, which for the purpose of this little exercise is all that is required—although to be honest I cannot think how you have escaped the clutches of some matchmaking mama for so long.'

'Just lucky, I guess. Of course, I don't have a title,' he said, his tongue firmly in his cheek, beginning to enjoy himself as the germ of an idea began to take hold, grow… 'Maybe that's the reason.'

'Two out of three isn't bad,' she pointed out. 'And you're bound to turn up in the New Year Honours sooner or later. So, what do you say, Mr Kavanagh, are you free this afternoon at two o'clock?'

Dear God, but the woman was cool. He wondered what it would take to heat her up. And would it be a slow overnight defrost, or was she the kind of woman who would simply explode in a rush of steam like a volcanic geyser?

'Where is this wedding?' he asked, to take his mind off such disturbing thoughts.

'St Margaret's.'

'St Margaret's, Westminster?'

'Fliss's mother is a Member of Parliament.'

'Formidable women run in the family, then?' His eyes creased in amusement.

'At least one in every generation,' she confirmed. Then, 'The reception is in Knightsbridge. We wouldn't have to stay late. In fact, if we appeared desperately keen to leave early it would be a positive bonus.' She lifted her shoulders in the most elegant of shrugs. 'My mother wouldn't bother me about biological clocks for months.'

Fergus sat back and regarded the lady with interest. Such quick thinking was rare, and he could well understand how she had made it to the boardroom at such an early age. But he wasn't slow on his feet when it came to taking advantage of unexpected opportunities. He might not want a ticket for the FA Cup Final, but Miss Veronica Grant had just offered him the perfect answer to his own difficulties.

'You have gone to great lengths to ask me for a favour, Miss Grant,' he said, 'and such quick thinking should not go unrewarded.'

'Is that a yes?' she enquired hopefully.

'A qualified yes. My top hat and brand-new morning suit are at your disposal this afternoon...'

Her smile was tinged with uncertainty. 'But—?' she added, after a small pause.

He returned her smile. He'd known she would understand. 'But,' he confirmed, 'I shall require a small favour in return.'

'Well, that's only fair,' she agreed, happy to indulge him in whatever sporting fantasy turned him on. 'What event did you have in mind?'

'Event?'

'A day at Lord's? The Centre Court on Finals Day at Wimbledon?'

'Could you manage even that?' he asked.

'It wouldn't be easy,' she admitted. 'But then, nothing worth the effort is ever easy.'

Fergus decided that Miss Grant was a woman with more than good looks to commend her. 'On this occasion it will be. That is, if you are free on the seventeenth of this month. It's a Saturday.'

'I'll make sure that I am,' she said, without hesitation, without even asking what he wanted in return. Gutsy as well as cool. Or maybe just desperate. Her mother must be right out of the boys' book of dragons.

'Then all I ask in return for my company this afternoon is that you don your wedding hat again and come to my sister's wedding as my guest.' He could see that she was puzzled. 'We'll form our own escort agency, you and I. A very exclusive one. I will keep at bay the suitors your mother has lined up for you; your task will be to fend off a gaggle of hopeful spinsters, widows and divorcees that Dora and Poppy have targeted as prospective wives for me.'

'You're joking!' she gasped.

'I sincerely wish I was,' he replied.

He'd overheard them quite by chance. He had been about to risk the dining room, which had become the centre of operations for wedding planning, and take the girls a drink to fortify them as they sorted out the final details, when Dora's voice had brought him up short.

'Ginnie Metcalfe would be the perfect wife for Gussie, you know. She's not too old for babies, but not so young that he'd look stupid. I can't bear old men with young wives, can you?' *Old? Thirty-eight wasn't old!* 'She's been brought up to run a big house and she's got the most wonderful seat on a horse.'

'Darling, Ginnie Metcalfe *looks* like a horse,' Poppy had replied, and the pair of them had dissolved into giggles. *Giggles!* It was not in the least bit amusing, and he'd been about to march in there and tell them so when Poppy had said, 'I think Sarah Darcy-Williams is our best bet. If you made her your matron of honour, you could sit her next to him at the reception.'

Sarah Darcy-Williams! Never. Not in a million years. Not if she was the last woman on earth.

'She's been married before,' Dora had said doubtfully. *And the poor guy had had to run for his life after two years. The mystery of it was how he had managed to stick it out for so long.* 'Of course, that does mean she'll have had the romance knocked out of her, and let's be honest, Poppy, Gussie isn't one of life's great romantics. I mean, can you imagine him sending a woman red roses?'

'Or silk underwear.'

'Silk underwear?' Dora had given a little whoop of

astonishment. 'Are you telling me that Richard buys you silk underwear?'

'Just a little something now and then, to wrap around a pair of earrings or a pendant...' This had been followed by a deep sigh from Poppy.

Romantic? When the hell had he had time to be romantic? Keeping one step ahead of them had taken every vestige of wit he possessed. Not that he was a total stranger to the florist, or to long-stemmed red roses come to that—but buying a woman silk underwear...? Maybe he was getting old, because he would have thought that was the quickest way to a black eye known to man, even if you were married to her.

While he'd pondered on the illogicality of women, his sisters had proceeded to dissect his character with the precision of a pair of brain surgeons as they matched him against every available female over the age of thirty in the county.

They'd clearly decided it was time he had a wife to take care of him now that they were both otherwise involved, and, quite overlooking the fact that he'd spent the last fifteen years looking after them, they'd decided that it was their duty to find him one. Someone sensible; someone who would be grateful for the attention; someone who had reached the magic age of thirty. He was sure it would have been older but for the fact that they were concerned that he might want an heir. Kind of them to be so considerate.

The trouble was that once those two girls had put their minds to something, nothing would move them. He could protest as much as he liked that he had no intention of marrying anyone, least of all any of the women *they* had picked out as likely candidates.

They would humour him, make a fuss of him, tell him not to worry about a thing, and if he wasn't extremely wary he would very shortly find himself standing at the altar of the village church, waiting for some female who would be wearing a vast amount of lace and a smile like the Cheshire Cat as she chained him to her with a tiny band of gold. It was quite possible that he would even be quite happy at the prospect. He'd seen it happen to more than one man. It was quite terrifying what women were capable of…

His only advantage was that they had no idea that he had wind of their plans. It wasn't much, but he intended to put it to good use. His first move was to take himself out of harm's way, somewhere safe, where he wouldn't find himself agreeing to some innocent-sounding invitation that would result in tears before bedtime. His tears.

And in the privacy of his club, a place where no one would be allowed to bother him without his express permission, he could spend the entire weekend in serious consideration of some way to divert them from their devious little plan.

Once the wedding was over, he would be safe. Dora would be on honeymoon with John, and when they returned she would have a husband, her little stepdaughter, Sophie, and all the distractions of everyday life, as well as her charity work to keep her busy. And Poppy's contract with an American cosmetic company would soon take her and Richard back across the Atlantic.

It was the week before the wedding that would be the most dangerous period. There would be any number of dinners and small parties for family and friends, affairs at which the Ginnie Metcalfes and Sarah Darcy-Williamses would be pushed at him with the belief firmly implanted by his sisters that, with a little effort, they might soon be Mrs Fergus Kavanagh. Rather like a game of pass the parcel—whoever caught him when the music stopped would be the winner. He wasn't a vain man, but he was well aware that he would make a prize catch for an ambitious woman.

Unaware of his sister's plans, he might just have been flattered enough by all the attention to slip a little…and where two or three determined women were gathered in the cause of matrimony, a slip was all it would take.

Of course, Veronica Grant was ambitious, too. She had to be to have broken through the glass ceiling and risen to the top in what was still largely a man's world. But she was ambitious on her own behalf. She was no more on the prowl for a wealthy husband than he was seeking a suitable wife, with or without a good seat on a horse.

She had taken him by surprise with her suggestion, it was true, but nobody had ever suggested he was slow in latching on to a good idea. She was, in fact, the answer to a confirmed bachelor's prayer.

And, like all the best plans, it had simplicity to commend it. It was delightfully simple. Perfectly simple. Fergus could hardly wait to see Poppy and Dora's reaction when they discovered that their dull, unromantic, boring old brother could find a woman of such elegance, self-assurance and beauty without any assistance from them.

Always assuming, of course, that Veronica Grant would agree to a double distraction. 'You need me to keep your mother's posse of prospective bridegrooms at bay and I'm happy to do it,' he said. 'All I ask in return is that you stick to my side like glue at Dora's wedding in two weeks' time. No strings. No complications. Not even the momentary embarrassment of a cheque in an envelope. Just two people helping each other out of a difficult situation.' He smiled at her across the remnants of their breakfast. 'Well, Miss Grant, what do you say? Do we have a deal?'

CHAPTER THREE

VERONICA had acted on an impulse born out of desperation when she'd seen Fergus Kavanagh sprinting across the platform and climbing aboard the train. But then, all her really good decisions had been made that way. Not that she would ever have admitted it. Women did not reach the boardroom by admitting to anything as unbusinesslike as 'feminine intuition', the distaff version of that old favourite 'gut instinct' so often used by men to justify decisions which seemed completely off the wall.

But it was one thing taking a chance on a business deal, quite another propositioning a man she had never met before on the eight-fifteen to London.

Looking across at him now, she could still scarcely credit that split-second quantum leap from idea to action. But a deep-down tingle as he had entered the carriage had told her that she had been right, that her intuition was in perfect working order. Fergus Kavanagh was, without doubt, the man to impress her mother: chiselled good looks, classic tailoring and the kind of financial stability that would stand up to any amount of scrutiny. It was a winning combination, and with him on her arm she would certainly be spared her mother's pointed references to the march of time.

She glanced at Kavanagh surreptitiously from beneath her lashes and discovered that he was watching her, waiting for her answer. By his own admission, he came into that category of thirty-something men who had somehow escaped marriage. Had he really been too busy to find a wife, or could it be that his interests lay in another direction? Could it be that he was in fact gay, but chose to keep the truth from his matchmaking sisters?

There was nothing in those thoughtful brown eyes to raise her pulse or her blood pressure, yet there was something, a stillness, that sent a warning tingle straight to her toes. If this had been a business meeting, she would have known he was the most dangerous man in the room, and up close, in full colour, Mr Fergus Kavanagh looked a great deal more impressive than his fuzzy newspaper photograph had suggested.

When he'd appeared in the doorway of the dining car she'd almost lost her nerve, unexpectedly daunted by the power that seemed to emanate from him; it was an unfamiliar feeling. She was used to being the one in control.

But now all she had to do was say ''yes'' and they would be conspirators. It would be them against the meddling matchmakers, and who could ever doubt that they would win?

The idea gave her the kind of buzz she got from a real business deal, the kind involving millions of pounds, and suddenly she wanted to laugh out loud. 'I say we have a deal, Mr Kavanagh,' she said.

'Fergus,' he said, offering her his strong, long-boned hand to seal the bargain. 'It had better be Fergus, don't you think?' Mischief sparked unexpectedly in the depths of those dark, still eyes. 'If we're to convince your mother, and anyone else who's interested, that we are lovers.'

Veronica felt her cheeks heat up. It was one thing making plans in her head. Quite another to look a perfect stranger in the face while he said the word out loud. Lovers. Of course, that was what she had intended her mother to believe and he knew it. They were, after all, a little mature just to be holding hands.

'Veronica,' she said quickly, rather than reply to his question, but as she accepted his hand she wished she hadn't thought of them holding hands in quite that way.

The tingle of awareness as skin touched skin, as his fingers closed about hers, was no figment of her imagination; there was an undeniable flare of excitement, of risk even, rare enough to trigger all kinds of built-in alarm systems. Not that they were necessary, she reminded herself. This was nothing more than a little mutual aid.

'Veronica,' he repeated.

'Or Ronnie, if you prefer.'

'Ronnie?'

'It's a nickname left over from school.' From the look on his face she should have abandoned it there, along with her gym slip and hockey stick.

'My sisters call me Gussie—when they think I can't hear them,' he admitted.

'Do they?' Her eyes widened. 'It doesn't suit you.'

'No more than Ronnie suits you.'

'Oh.' She had the feeling that something less formal would have been more appropriate if they had been lovers, but could not quite bring herself to say so. 'Well, most people find my name rather a mouthful and try to shorten it.'

'That's no reason to make it easy for them. Veronica suits you. It's a lovely name.'

She stared at him for a moment, unable to quite decipher his tone of voice. Was that a compliment? His face gave nothing away. She suspected that it never would...unless he wanted it to. She looked up, grateful for the interruption, as the steward approached with the bill for breakfast, quickly putting some money on the plate in order to forestall Kavanagh's offer to pay for hers.

Having hijacked him, she knew she should offer to pay for both of them, but he would certainly refuse to allow her to do that, and she had no wish to cause any unnecessary awkwardness between them. It was beginning to occur to her that the possibilities for that were already legion. Instead, she looked out of the window at the bleak concrete retaining walls that lined the last mile or so of the track into London. 'We're nearly there.'

'Where are you going? If we're heading in the same direction, we could share a taxi.'

She turned back to face him. 'I'm staying with a friend near Sloane Square. Just off the King's Road.'

'Is she going to the wedding, too?'

'Well, yes—'

'Then it might be a good idea if she sees us together,' Fergus said. 'What's her name?'

'Suzie Broughton, but I thought you had an urgent appointment with your tailor.'

'He'll wait.' Irritating his tailor was a small price to pay for the enjoyment of this highly original woman's company for a few more minutes. 'As a matter of interest, what would you have done if I hadn't been about to pick up a morning suit?'

'Nothing.' She smiled as his eyebrows rose in surprise. 'I'm sure you're more than capable of renting one without any help from me. If not, you wouldn't be the man for the job.'

There was no answer to that. Or, at least, not one that immediately leapt to mind. Instead, he stood up and took his overnight bag from the rack. 'Is this yours?' he asked, turning to the Vuitton case. Without waiting for an answer, he lifted it down and stood it alongside his, remaining on his feet as the train slid into the station. 'You know, it has occurred to me that we should spend a little time getting our stories straight. Where we met—that sort of thing. It wouldn't do to contradict one another. If your mother is the least bit suspicious—'

'Why should she be?' She stood up, easing her lovely legs from beneath the table. She was tall, five-ten at least, and her dark, pencil-slim skirt stopped a long way short of her knees. She slid her arms into a matching jacket that skimmed her hips and stopped a few inches short of the hem of her skirt.

'She sounds like the type of woman who takes a keen interest in your affairs,' he said, more to distract himself from her legs than for any genuine concern that they would be found out.

Veronica grinned. 'If you mean nosy, Fergus, just say so. You won't be far from the truth.' He simply smiled, deep creases adding character and warmth to his face, but he had a point. The potential for disaster suddenly seemed endless, and she looked up at him.

'Are you quite sure you want to go ahead with this?' she asked. 'I should warn you that she's a hard woman to fool, and I'd really hate to cause you any embarrassment.'

'Don't worry about it, Veronica. I've brought up two younger sisters; I'm impossible to embarrass. Besides, I am at least as eager for your aid as you are for mine, possibly more so. If you knew Dora and Poppy, you'd understand why,' he added feelingly. 'Why don't we take time out for coffee and I'll tell you all about them?' She didn't exactly leap at the offer, Fergus noticed. 'Or perhaps you're too busy this morning?'

Veronica was old enough to recognise when she was being offered an escape route. Fergus Kavanagh looked every inch a gentleman, and clearly he had the instincts of the breed. Her hesitation was unworthy of him. Unworthy of her. 'I'd love to, but once I've dropped my things off at Suzie's I have to get to the hairdresser's.'

He felt the desperate urge to say something absolutely crass, such as her hair was perfect already, but he restrained himself. If the lady believed she needed a hairdresser, he was well aware that nothing on earth would convince her otherwise. Instead, he smiled reassuringly. 'It's not a problem. We'll simply parry all awkward questions with an enigmatic smile.'

'I don't think that will work on my mother.'

'You'd be surprised. If she quizzes me, just follow my lead.' She looked doubtful. 'It'll be fine.' She was rocked against him as the train came to a standstill, and as Fergus held her arm briefly to steady her, her scent seemed to steal over him. Sophisticated, cool, distinctively floral. He searched his memory in an attempt to place the flower, but for the moment it eluded him… 'Just fine,' he repeated.

'If you say so. It's a little late to exchange detailed biographies, although maybe we should have a mutual exchange of faxes before your sister's wedding?' she offered.

Putting a stop to any suggestion that they might meet and get their stories straight in the meantime?

Maybe.

But he didn't argue. Her swift move to forestall any move he might have made to pay for her breakfast had not gone unnoticed, and she had stooped to pick up her bag before he could do it for her. Miss Veronica Grant was clearly a lady who took equality seriously.

Then Peter appeared with her hatbox, and Fergus was able to demonstrate his own commitment to equality—at least to the extent that he was unfazed by such feminine trivia. Poppy and Dora had knocked all that rubbish out of him long ago.

'Thank you, Peter, I'll take that.' He exchanged the hatbox for a discreetly palmed banknote. 'Have a pleasant weekend.'

'And you, sir.'

'Are you going to see the Rovers play on Saturday?' he asked.

'Never miss a game, sir,' Peter replied, without batting an eyelid. 'Goodbye, Miss Grant.'

'Goodbye, Peter. I'll be in touch.'

'What an old rogue,' Fergus said as they crossed the platform to the taxi rank.

Veronica laughed. 'Don't be hard on him. He probably thinks he's playing Cupid.' Even as she said the words she wished she could call them back, but whether he hadn't heard her above the noise and bustle of the station, the loudspeaker announcements, or whether he had decided it would be wiser not to respond, Fergus simply opened the cab door for her and stood back to let her climb aboard.

'Chelsea,' he said, glancing back at Veronica. She supplied the address and he closed the door and folded himself into the seat alongside her.

'Are you really sure about this, Fergus?' Veronica turned to him as the driver eased the cab out of the station and into the traffic. 'If you wanted to change your mind, I would quite understand.'

'After all the trouble you've gone to? Not to mention parting with a ticket to the most important sporting occasion of the year.'

'Only if you're a football fan,' she pointed out, looking away again.

'Veronica?' She seemed to be transfixed by the back of the cab driver's head. 'You're not really getting cold feet about this?'

'No, but—'

But? But what? She was the answer to his own personal prayer and he wasn't going to let her get away now. 'Then it must be something else. Could it be that, on closer inspection, you have decided that I'm not quite up to your mother's high standards?' he enquired.

For the second time that morning a blush tinged her cheeks as, horrified, she swung round to face him and declared, 'Good heavens, no! You're absolutely perfect.' The blush, if anything, deepened. 'If we had more time to get our story straight. But—'

He'd had enough of 'buts'. 'Perfect? I don't believe that anyone has ever called me that before,' he said, before she could think of some other reason why they should call the whole thing off. He'd seen her face when she'd realised that mentioning Cupid had been a serious mistake, and he was beginning to suspect that the cool blonde was not quite as cool as she would have him believe. It made her boldness all the more interesting.

Of course, it could just be that, having hijacked him with all the subtlety of a double-glazing salesman with his foot in the door, she now felt obliged to give him a chance to change his mind. The personal equivalent of the 'statutory cooling off period'. It was generous of her, but he was not about to take advantage of her offer; once she was in his debt he was certain that she would keep her side of the bargain, and her presence at his side was beginning to make the prospect of Dora's wedding positively enjoyable.

'Then that's settled. Now, we have as long as it takes the driver to reach Sloane Square to make up some delightful nonsense about how we met...unless you'd rather be utterly outrageous and tell the truth?'

'The truth?'

'That you bribed the dining car steward on the eight-fifteen to sit me at your table and then proceeded to proposition me quite shamelessly?'

'It's a thought,' Veronica replied, with a swift sideways glance.

'It has the advantage that no one in their right mind would believe it,' he pointed out.

Veronica was used to being in control, but it seemed that Fergus was too. She didn't think she should make it quite that easy for him. 'I don't think I'm prepared to take the risk. But we could try it on your sisters if you like,' she offered.

Fergus grinned. 'Ouch.'

'Any time.'

'So, how *did* we meet?'

'Well, I suppose it's quite plausible that we should have met on a train coming up to town,' she pointed out. 'You do it regularly; I do it at least a couple of times a month.'

'Over breakfast?'

Veronica had a very strong suspicion that Fergus Kavanagh was teasing her. She refused to be teased. 'Why not? I usually have breakfast on the train,' she said boldly. 'And, since we both live near Melchester, what could be more natural than that we should meet again at somewhere of mutual interest?' She paused, waiting for him to offer a suggestion.

'At a concert?'

'You're a music lover?'

'I'm a patron of Melchester City Orchestra.'

'That's keen,' she admitted.

'Or the museum? Have you seen the Kavanagh Room?'

She hadn't, but there had been a piece in the local newspaper when it had been opened recently. 'The one with all those bits of Greek pot?' she offered.

'Sherds,' he corrected. 'Potsherds.' Then, 'My mother was an archaeologist. She left her "bits of pot" and her papers to the museum along with the money to house them. It's taken a while to build, but the new annexe is worth a visit.' He paused. 'If you like bits of pot.' She wasn't sure whether she was supposed to laugh or not, he realised. 'What are your interests, Veronica?' he asked, rescuing her.

'I visit friends. Ride when I have the opportunity—' Fergus smiled. 'What?'

He shook his head. 'Nothing, it's just something Dora said...' He stopped as the taxi turned a corner and drew up in front of a small but charming house. 'We appear to have arrived.' He opened the cab door, helped her out and then carried her hatbox and suitcase to the front door, where he put down the suitcase and proceeded to ring the bell.

'There's really no need to wait,' Veronica said.

'I thought we'd already agreed that I was a gentleman,' he replied. 'Suppose your friend is not at home? You'd be left on the doorstep with your luggage.'

'Suzie's expecting me.'

'Any one of a number of emergencies might have called her from home,' he pointed out.

'Suzie does not have emergencies—' she began, and as if to confirm her words there was the sound of footsteps approaching the door. 'You see?'

'I do.' And he offered her the hatbox.

'Thank you,' she said, taking it.

'It was my pleasure.' And once her hands were fully occupied he leaned forward to cradle her cheek lightly in the curve of his palm. 'In fact, I can't remember when I've enjoyed a journey on the eight-fifteen more.'

Her eyes widened in surprise, but she didn't move, and as the door began to open he bent to kiss her lightly on the mouth. He could have warned her, he probably should have warned her, but he knew that she would have instinctively backed off so that the impact would have been lost.

She might believe it would be easy to fool her friends that they were lovers. He was not a man to leave such things to chance; the briefest of kisses would convince far more than words. At least, he had intended the briefest of kisses. Somehow it didn't quite turn out quite that way.

Veronica might appear as cool as frosting on a glass, but her lips were unexpectedly warm, offering the kind of welcome a man would be hard put to it to refuse; it was the kind of heat that came from inside, simmering on hold, waiting for the right moment to boil over.

It was like eating hot ice cream. Sweet. Unexpected. Something he had to try again just to be sure that his senses were not playing tricks on him.

They were not playing tricks, and, as the kiss went on and on, he knew the answer to the question he had pondered earlier on the train. There would be no slow, overnight defrost with this lady. She was definitely a volcano. Dormant, perhaps. Snow-capped, even. But beneath that serene surface he was convinced lay a molten core. And as he finally, reluctantly, straightened, to look down into a pair of startled silvery eyes, he had a fleeting impression that until that moment she had not been aware of it herself.

He closed the hand he had laid against her cheek, grazing it briefly with his knuckles before turning to smile at the young woman standing open-mouthed in the doorway.

'Hello,' he said, offering his hand, 'you must be

Suzie. Fergus Kavanagh.' Suzie Broughton, for once in her life utterly speechless, allowed her fingers to linger in his. 'Forgive me for dropping Veronica and running, but I should be somewhere else right now.' He turned back to Veronica. She had not moved, quite possibly had not breathed, since he had kissed her. Rather the way *he* had felt when she had dropped her little bombshell in the train. They should be even. Except that his own oxygen intake wasn't quite what it should be. 'I'll pick you up here at one-thirty,' he told her, and, without waiting for a reply, he turned and walked quickly down the steps.

'Who was *that*?' Suzie demanded as the cab pulled away from the kerb.

Veronica regarded Suzie's wide eyes and eager expression with a sinking feeling. When she asked, 'Who was *that*?' she didn't mean his name. Fergus had introduced himself, so she already knew his name. What Suzie wanted was a rundown of his family background, details of his eligibility, preferably with a copy of his bank statement attached, and every last detail of their relationship from the moment they'd first met until this very minute.

Suzie Broughton had been her very best friend from the day they had started nursery school together, and she considered such information to be her right.

Veronica groaned inwardly. What on earth had she done? She had to be crazy to think she could get away with this kind of deception.

Then she considered the alternative. Being endlessly polite to the procession of Hooray Henrys her mother would have starred on the guest list—a guest list provided by the bride's mother for that express purpose—as likely husband material.

No. This was not the moment for an attack of faint-heartedness. Besides, if she could fool Suzie, she could certainly fool her mother and the legion of aunts and cousins who would undoubtedly have been drafted in to remind her at every conceivable opportunity that time was marching on.

'Well?' Suzie demanded, when she didn't immediately reply.

'You mean you don't know?' Veronica asked, with every appearance of surprise, as she handed her friend the hatbox to keep her busy, and give herself a few seconds for thought while she retrieved her suitcase from the doorstep. 'I'm shocked, Suz. I thought you were up to speed on every eligible bachelor this side of Hadrian's Wall.' Then she grinned. 'Both sides of it, come to think of it.'

'I am. Or I thought I was. That one seems to have escaped me. I can't think how. He's...well, he's—' For the second time in five minutes Suzie was quite lost for words.

'Yes, isn't he?' Veronica concluded helpfully. 'Of course, he lives in Melchester, like me. Right out in the sticks.'

'Even so,' Suzie murmured, oblivious to being teased.

'And I have to admit that he's more likely to be featured in the *Financial Times* than *Hello!* magazine.' Then, 'He has two sisters,' she said, offering a clue.

'Do I know *them*?'

'I've no idea. Poppy?' she offered. 'Dora?'

Veronica could almost see the cogs of Suzie's mind working as she matched the names against the punch cards of her memory. Her forehead creased as she said, 'Kavanagh?' Then she shook her head. 'You can't mean Poppy and Dora Kavanagh.'

'Can't I?'

'But their brother is—' And then she answered her own question. 'Oh, God.' Suzie clapped her hand to her mouth. 'Don't tell me that was *the* Fergus Kavanagh?' Veronica obliged. 'But he must be one of the most elusive bachelors in England.'

'Not *that* elusive.' Suzie was seriously impressed. Which was good. And bad. If he was that much of a catch there would be a lot more interest than she had bargained on. Than he had bargained on, too, no doubt. 'Just too busy making a living for idle socialising, I imagine.'

'Making a living?' Suzie was too astonished to take offence at her friend's remark. '*Making a living?* Are you crazy, Ronnie? The man's middle name is Midas. Everything he touches—' She seemed momentarily lost for words. 'What a catch!'

Veronica chose not to confirm or deny whether Fergus Kavanagh had, indeed, been caught. She merely smiled. 'There, you see? Easy, wasn't it? You didn't need my help at all. Do you know Poppy Kavanagh?' she enquired, as if she herself had known the woman for years, in an attempt to sidetrack Suzie at least temporarily.

'Everyone knows her. Or at least knows *of* her. She signed that contract as the face of some American cosmetic firm last year and she's married to Richard Marriott. They say it was love at first sight.'

'Do they?' Suzie's knowledge of the social scene was legendary, whilst she, like Fergus, was too busy working to bother keeping up.

'And Dora Kavanagh's been running supplies to refugee camps in…' She flapped her hand vaguely as she tried to remember exactly where, before giving up. 'Oh, I don't know. Somewhere.' Suzie was getting into her stride now. 'And *she's* about to marry John Gannon, that journalist who spent months hunting for his daughter and then nearly ended up in jail when he smuggled her into the country. You must have seen him on television. I wept buckets…' On reflection, Veronica realised that she had. And shed a tear or two of her own. It seemed that, whilst her own perusal of the *Financial Times* might have given her some background information about Kavanagh Industries, Suzie, who was addicted to the diary pages, knew a great deal more about the life history of Fergus Kavanagh, or at least his family, than she did. 'But why am I telling you?' Suzie said. 'You must have been invited.'

'Yes,' she said. 'I've been invited. The wedding is in two weeks.'

Suzie's eyes gleamed as she scented a story. 'Does this mean that you and Fergus are…?' She left Veronica to fill in the blank.

Veronica realised that it was time to change the subject before Suzie could get fully into her inquisitorial stride. 'Darling, will the gossip keep for a few minutes? If my dress isn't hung up immediately I'll look a total mess this afternoon.'

There was a disbelieving grunt, but she didn't object. 'You know which room.' The one good thing about Suzie was that she had her priorities right. Clothes first. Then gossip. 'I'll make some coffee while you're freshening up, and then we can have a really good chat.'

'Lovely,' Veronica said, then added, 'I can't wait to hear all *your* news.'

Upstairs, she opened her small suitcase, shaking out the dress she had bought for the wedding and hanging it over the wardrobe door. Then she laid out her toiletries, washed her hands and checked her hair in the mirror. But her eyes seemed to be transfixed by her mouth.

She lifted her hand and with just the tips of her fingers touched her lips, so recently, so unexpectedly, so thoroughly kissed. Not gay. Definitely not gay.

All through that conversation with Suzie she had been conscious of the heat left by his mouth, the tingle where his knuckles had grazed her cheek.

She should be cross at such a brazen move on his part. He should have discussed it with her…asked…

Then she found herself grinning idiotically at her reflection as she considered how they might have choreographed the moves in the back of the taxi as it had crawled through the morning traffic. It would have amused the taxi driver. It could quite conceivably have caused an accident… She let the image go. No. It would never have worked. They would have been far too self-conscious, or at least *she* would have been self-conscious. She wasn't so sure about Fergus…

She had wished for an adventurer, and so far he had more than lived up to the billing, establishing their relationship far more convincingly than any story they could have invented in such a short time.

Suzie would be breaking her neck to tell people how they had arrived on her doorstep together that morning, that Fergus had been kissing her when she opened the door. And there could be no suggestion that either of them had been faking it…

She snatched back her fingers, found her lipstick and set about repairing the damage, determined to put the incident out of her mind. Not that the cool gloss could quite eradicate the warm, throbbing tingle. Her newly painted lips seemed to glow right back at her from the mirror.

Had Fergus *really* been thinking that far ahead?

She straightened her collar. Obviously. Why else would he kiss her?

But had it required quite such enthusiasm? And did he always do everything with such thoroughness?

She smoothed down her skirt.

Of course he did. His reputation guaranteed it. Fergus Kavanagh was a man to be reckoned with, and not just in business. Her instincts had not let her down. The fact that her eyes were suspiciously bright and there was a faint flush to her cheeks that hadn't been there this morning was proof enough of that.

But she had a more pressing problem than the fact that Fergus Kavanagh was a nine-out-of-ten man when it came to kissing. Quite possibly ten-out-of-ten, given a little more time and somewhere rather more promising than a doorstep…

CHAPTER FOUR

SUZIE. Incorrigibly curious and harder to distract than a wasp at a picnic, her best friend Suzie would want every last detail of their supposed relationship. Veronica glanced at her watch. Or maybe not.

It was just after ten-thirty. If she could get through coffee without giving the game away, she would be able to escape to the safety of the hairdresser's. After that they would both be too busy getting ready for the wedding to indulge in intimate girl talk. And if, rather than stay overnight, she invented some reason why she simply had to return to Melchester tonight, she would be home and dry.

No problem.

She flicked back her hair.

Nothing to worry about.

After the way she had picked up Fergus Kavanagh this morning, she could handle anything. Even Suzie in gossip overdrive. But as she smiled at her reflection, her lips seemed to mock her.

Downstairs, Suzie was in the kitchen putting the finishing touches to the tray, and she looked up as Veronica walked in. 'I thought we might have coffee outside, take advantage of this lovely weather.'

Veronica was not fooled by her friend's apparent loss of interest in Fergus Kavanagh. 'Great. Here, let me take that.' And she picked up the tray, carrying it through to a tiny courtyard garden filled with old stone and terracotta pots from which tulips and forget-me-nots and aubretia tumbled in a riot of late spring colour.

Veronica put the tray down on the table while Suzie shooed a small grey cat from one of the chairs. 'It's so lovely to see you, Ronnie. You never come to town since you moved to Melchester.'

'Yes, I do. At least twice a month.'

'Oh, for work. Not play. That doesn't count.' She patted her bottom and pulled a face. 'I haven't been to the gym for weeks without you to keep me up to scratch. I've no self-discipline.'

'It doesn't show.' Veronica doubted that Suzie could stay away from the gossip palace of the gym any more than she could fly. 'But why don't you and Nigel come and stay for a few days now the weather is so much warmer? I've finally decorated my spare bedroom, and the countryside around Melchester is very pretty. There are some lovely walks along the river,' she added mischievously.

'Walks?' Suzie looked horrified.

'There's a country park quite near, too.'

'You must be joking! A gentle stroll around Harvey Nicks is about my limit. You know me, Ronnie, I'm addicted to city pavements...trees *scare* me.'

'London is full of trees,' Veronica pointed out.

'I know, but they're the domesticated, *restrained* kind of trees that know their place. Out there in the countryside, well...I'd rather not risk it.' She paused. 'Everyone was stunned when you decided to sell up and move out of London, you know.'

So that was the way Suzie was going to play it;

start with what she knew and work outwards. 'Haven't we had this conversation before?' she asked.

'I know, but I still don't understand. You worked so hard to build up your own company—'

'A fact that was reflected in the price I sold it for.' She thought Suzie had understood all that, but if it kept the conversation away from Fergus she was quite happy to explain it all again, at length. 'The lease was up on my flat, Suzie, and there were sound business reasons for selling my company.' And she was a businesswoman. 'It was time to decide where I was headed. Did I want to be in the same place in five years' time?'

'You could have been married, been a countess, Ronnie—'

'A title is not a reason for getting married, Suz. I haven't yet met a man worth changing my life for.' It was a story that had worked since the split with George; she could see no reason to change it.

'Not even Fergus Kavanagh?'

'You're beginning to sound like my mother,' she warned.

'Good grief, am I?' And Suzie, perhaps realising that she'd gone just a little too far, laughed and let it go. 'That will never do. After all, you always knew what you wanted, where you were going.'

'So did you. You wanted to leave school and marry Nigel.'

'While you were clearly never meant to hang on to the coat tails of some man.' She broke off a piece of biscuit and dropped it for the cat. 'You always were the ambitious one, Ronnie. Even at kindergarten everything you did was gold star material.'

'Rubbish. Besides, ambition isn't always enough. Success requires capital. The marketing company had gone just about as far as I could take it on my own, and companies are like people, they have to grow or stagnate and wither. Sooner or later I would have been swallowed up by a much bigger organisation and just become a little fish in some great big pond.'

'I doubt that. You'd have been running the place in five years.'

'Only if I was prepared to spend more time playing internal politics than doing my job. Not my scene, Suz.'

Suzie shuddered in sympathy. 'I'd hate it.'

Veronica thought Suzie would be thoroughly at home playing power politics in a big company, but she held her peace. If Suzie wanted explanations, she would get explanations. It meant less time fending off questions about Fergus.

'I had an offer for the business from someone wanting to expand quickly, someone who had the backing to move into the really big time. I was working on a project at Jefferson's at the time, and when Nick Jefferson offered me a seat on the board, well...' she spread her hands in an eloquent gesture '...that was it.'

'But don't you *miss* London?' *London? The suffocating circle of friends who always appeared to be on the point of asking the question, but who never quite dared? She couldn't wait to get away. It was why she hated these major social occasions. The look she always saw in the eyes of her friends, her family. She had offered no explanation and neither had George, and no one had ever been quite brave enough to ask. But it didn't stop them wondering.*

'Melchester is not the end of the world, you know. It's a city—a small city, I grant you, but it's a great place to live. No traffic jams, no pollution, at least not by London standards. Why don't you come and see for yourself? We have an orchestra, an art gallery, a museum,' she added, in homage to Fergus.

'Oh, *wow*.'

'And a very elegant shopping mall in the atrium of the Jefferson Tower.'

Suzie gave her a sly grin. 'And of course Marlowe Court is quite near Melchester.'

'Marlowe Court?'

'Fergus Kavanagh's estate?' Suzie reminded her teasingly. *Marlowe Court? That was where he lived? That beautiful old stone manor house a few miles outside the city? She'd passed it a couple of times*... 'Tell me, did you meet Fergus Kavanagh *before* or *after* this fabulous offer from Nick Jefferson?'

'What? Oh, after,' she answered swiftly, when she realised that Suzie was grinning idiotically. 'That is quite a recent development.'

Her friend was not discouraged. 'And now he's coming to Fliss's wedding with you?'

'He was coming to town anyway,' she pointed out. 'It's no big deal.'

'No? You mean you hadn't planned to introduce him to your mother on neutral territory?'

'How do you know my mother hasn't already met him?'

'Because, my dearest friend, I would have heard. Everyone would have heard. And everyone would have been talking about it. I can't wait to see how he handles the moment of truth.' Veronica raised her eyebrows. 'That moment when he discovers that your mother's dearest ambition is to marry you off to some wealthy aristocrat.'

'Fergus isn't an aristocrat, so he's nothing to worry about, and he's quite capable of handling my mother.'

'He can certainly handle you.' She grinned. 'Kissing on the doorstep like a pair of lovebirds... I never thought I'd see the day...' Neither had she, but Veronica refused to rise to her friend's teasing. 'So, are you going to tell me all the lovely details of this affair, or am I going to have to extract them from you with tweezers?'

'Affair? I don't remember saying anything about an affair.'

'Of course,' she carried on as if Veronica hadn't spoken, 'if you don't want to tell me about it, just say so. I'll understand. I'll hate you, but I'll understand.'

'There's nothing to tell, Suz. Fergus and I...' It was definitely time to be enigmatic, mysterious, understated. She paused tantalisingly. 'Are just good friends.' Not even that. Acquaintances. *Kissing acquaintances.*

'Oh, I *see*. It's *that* serious.' And Suzie smiled like a cat who'd just been locked in the larder with a poached salmon. 'Help yourself to a biscuit.' Veronica shook her head. 'You're inhuman,' her friend groaned. 'You've no vices.'

She declined to comment on that, instead sipping her coffee before attempting a diversion. 'How's Nigel?' she asked.

'Overworked and overweight,' Suzie sighed. 'Much

the same as usual, in fact. And don't think I'll allow you to change the subject that easily. Where did you two meet?'

It was Veronica's turn to sigh a little. 'You're incorrigible, do you know that?'

Suzie grinned. 'You can't distract *me* with flattery, Veronica Grant. I'm a seeker after truth, the whole truth and nothing but the truth, and I won't rest until I have it.'

'Don't quote the gossips' charter at me,' Veronica warned her, grinning right back. 'Have one of those biscuits instead; it will keep your mouth busy.'

Suzie didn't need a second invitation, but it didn't keep her quiet. 'I met Poppy Kavanagh once at a charity thingie. Now, *she's* incorrigible, if you like. Did you know that she moved in with Richard Marriott the day she met him?'

'That's not incorrigible, Suzie, that's knowing what you want and not giving a damn who knows it.'

'Well, she got it.'

'So you said. That's love at first sight for you.'

'Dora fell for John Gannon like a ton of bricks too, or so I'm reliably told.'

'Perhaps it runs in the family,' Veronica suggested, and immediately knew she had made a mistake as Suzie's eyes lit up like Christmas.

'Is that how it was with you and Fergus?' she demanded, jumping in with both feet. 'Another case of love at first sight?'

'There was an instant rapport,' Veronica admitted, with a small smile.

'Really?' You just couldn't overdo enigmatic, apparently, because Suzie's face was positively glowing.

'It *must* be a family thing, then.' She bit into the biscuit and waited for more details. When Veronica didn't oblige, she said, 'His parents were inseparable too. They were into archaeology, or at least Mrs Kavanagh was, and her husband just adored her; he wouldn't let her go anywhere without him. They were killed in an earthquake somewhere.' She waved her hand vaguely. 'I'm not much good at geography.'

'You have other talents.'

Suzie grinned, unoffended. 'Fergus had just come down from Oxford. He couldn't have been more than twenty-two or three...' She paused to think.

'It was the year after he graduated,' Veronica dropped in, without shame. In fact, she was beginning to enjoy herself.

'He just took charge of everything. The company, the estate, his pre-teen sisters. Dora must have been quite small...' She turned to Veronica. 'But of course you know all that.'

Veronica smiled back. She'd known some of it. Most of it. The extra little details were interesting, more than interesting, but she wasn't going to get herself all tangled up with them. 'I can see you've been doing your homework while I've been unpacking,' she said, her voice all mock reproach. 'Who did you ring?'

'No one. It wasn't necessary. Once I've got a name,' she said, clicking her fingers, 'I have instant recall.'

'Do you?' The surprise was not feigned. 'That's odd. I don't remember you ever demonstrating this astonishing gift at school.'

'The only people they talked about at school had

been dead for centuries.' Suzie picked up another thin biscuit coated in dark Belgian chocolate and regarded it thoughtfully for a moment, before taking a small bite and letting it melt on her tongue. 'Come on, Ronnie. You're my best friend; I've known you for ever... And Fergus Kavanagh has the reputation of a man whose bachelorhood is set in concrete. Rather like your own, come to think of it. So when are you going to quit stalling and tell me?'

'Tell you what?'

'Everything. Come on, Ronnie,' Suzie demanded, impatient at her lengthy silence. 'I want every last detail. What's he like in bed?'

'Suzie!' she exclaimed, the colour flooding without warning into her cheeks. Highly convincing stuff, if Suzie's delighted chuckle was anything to go by.

This was like that old game they had played as children...what was it called? Truth, Dare, Kiss or Promise. This morning she had dared everything when she had waylaid Fergus; they had promised to help one another out of their mutual difficulties; Suzie was a determined searcher after truth, and an occasional kiss was to be expected—hoped for, even...

'All right, let's start with something easy and work up to the good stuff,' Suzie continued impatiently. 'Where did you meet him?'

Veronica's hand had strayed once more to her mouth. At Suzie's words she quickly dropped it, came back from that doorstep kiss. If this was a game, it was time she started concentrating and playing in earnest.

'Where did we meet?' At least she had an easy one for openers. They had already decided that it would be simpler to stick to the truth. But that didn't mean it couldn't be interesting. 'Over breakfast.'

Suzie, hand poised to take another biscuit, turned and stared. 'Over *breakfast*?'

'Mmm.' Veronica raised her cup to her lips. 'He likes kippers,' she said. 'And white toast. And coffee.' As she took a sip from her own cup, a wicked little urge prompted her to add, 'He has them every morning.'

Suzie's eyes widened. '*Every* morning?'

'Every morning,' she confirmed—hadn't Fergus said as much?

'That's...' Suzie loss of words was reaching epidemic proportions. But it didn't last for long. 'Indecent,' she finished.

'Is it? And I would have sworn that kippers were one of the few fishy delicacies that could not, under any circumstances, be described as indecent.' Slightly eccentric, perhaps.

'It depends upon the context,' Suzie said with feeling.

Veronica smiled. 'You're just a jealous old married woman,' she said, replacing her cup on the tray.

'Too true. Tell me more.'

'I'd love to stay and tell you every intimate detail,' she replied, without a trace of shame, 'but I really haven't got time. The traffic is horrendous this morning and Luigi's expecting me at eleven-thirty.' She rose to her feet with the most expressive of shrugs.

'Ronnie! You can't leave me like this,' Suzie wailed.

'You made the appointment for me yourself, Suz, and you know he'll throw a tantrum if I'm late.'

'Blame me! No one will see your hair under a hat!'

'But I'll know.' And she smiled, knowing that Suzie didn't really mean it.

'I can't believe you're going to run out on me now,' she muttered, reaching for the compensation of yet another chocolate biscuit.

Veronica, beginning to find it difficult to resist the need for chocolate herself, moved out of temptation's reach. 'You don't want me arriving at St Margaret's looking a mess, do you?'

'You have never looked a mess in your entire life. That's something else I'll never forgive you for.'

'If you'd seen me when I was decorating the spare bedroom you wouldn't say that.'

'Oh, sure. I bet you didn't get so much as a splash of paint on your pinny,' Suzie sulked.

Veronica laughed. 'You know that's not true. And we'll catch up later, I promise.' She stopped, remembering her escape plan. 'Although actually—'

'What?'

'I won't be able to stay tonight after all, Suzie.' She wanted to get this wedding over and get out of town as quickly as she could. 'I have to get back to Melchester. Something's come up—'

'It's all right, Ronnie, you don't have to explain,' Suzie said gravely. 'I quite understand.'

'Do you?' She was surprised. She'd expected a minor tantrum at the very least.

'Of course I do. Fergus can't be expected to go without his, umm, kippers.' As Veronica felt her cheeks begin to heat once more at her friend's interpretation of her excuse, Suzie reached out and took her hand. 'I'm sorry, I shouldn't tease. I do want you to be happy—'

Her sincerity was so obvious that Veronica felt an almost overwhelming urge to confess, tell her the truth. Suzie would understand. She would help, even. But she would not be able to resist telling her husband. That was the way of the world. What would married life be without a little pillow talk, after all?

Unfortunately, that wouldn't be the end of it. Nigel was a dear, but he just wouldn't be able to stop himself from passing on this hilarious piece of gossip in the changing room at his squash club.

And inevitably it would get back to her mother, who would never forgive her for making a fool of her, for playing games, wasting opportunities when the serious business of matchmaking was afoot.

Fergus Kavanagh didn't go to his club after all. Once he'd picked up his morning suit from his tailor, chosen a new shirt and cravat to go with it and borrowed a top hat, he headed for his office.

'Good morning, Julie.'

His personal assistant looked up from her desk and smiled. 'Hello, Fergus. What's the matter with Melchester today?'

'Nothing that the absence of my sisters wouldn't instantly put right.' They had worked together since he was a wet-behind-the-ears graduate with a company to drag back from the brink and she was an empty-nester looking for a new career once her children had flown.

He'd chosen her over the leggy blondes the Personnel Department had hoped would distract him, keep him out of everyone's hair so that they could carry on as they always had. Long lunches, long weekends and not a lot happening in between.

They had made their mistakes together in the early days, covered for each other, and now she was his firm right hand, with a staff of her own and a salary to match.

She grinned sympathetically. 'Are Dora's wedding preparations getting on top of you?' Her wedding preparations for him.

'You could say that.'

'Coffee, then,' she said, getting up to make it herself. 'Do you want to see the post?'

'Is there anything you can't handle?'

She grinned. 'No, I was just being polite.'

'That'll be the day. Just organise sandwiches for me for twelve-thirty. I'm going to a wedding and I don't want my stomach to rumble in church.' He caught her eye and grinned back. 'I know. I'm a glutton for punishment.'

'You said it.'

'And I'll need a car with a driver for one o'clock. Something roomy enough to accommodate a large hat.'

She glanced at the top hat he was holding. 'Yours?' she enquired. 'Or something wider?'

'The kind of hat that comes in a hatbox this big,' he said, making a broad angler's gesture. 'And then I want all the information you can dig up on Veronica Grant. She's on the board of Jefferson Sports. They're based in Melchester.' He paused in the doorway to his office, about to add that it was urgent, but she was already reaching for the telephone. He realised, too late, that he should have asked Veronica whose wedding they were going to. 'Have you got today's newspaper?'

She tucked it beneath his arm before he had finished speaking, and, closing the door behind him with his foot, he dropped his overnight bag on the floor, hooked his suit over the coatstand and tossed the remainder of his purchases along with the top hat onto a chair. Then he opened the newspaper at the 'Court & Social' page and spread it on his desk in order to peruse the list of the day's weddings.

Miss Felicity Wetherall to Viscount Carteret at St Margaret's, Westminster. That had to be the one. He pressed the button on the intercom. 'Julie, one more thing. Will you call my club and tell them I'll be staying there tonight?' Now that he had an ace up his sleeve in the form of Miss Veronica Grant, he wouldn't be needing a long-term hideout.

'No problem. If anyone wants you in the meantime, are you available?'

He glanced at his watch. 'No. I'm going to take a shower and change.'

'Well, don't forget to wash behind your ears.'

'One of these days you'll go too far, Julie.'

'I'm twenty years too old for that,' she replied. 'More's the pity.'

He showered and changed in the private suite attached to his office, and then, while he ate the sandwiches Julie had provided, he read the information that she had collated for him from the financial pages. She'd done a good job in the time, but there was little that he didn't already know.

They told him that Veronica Grant was beautiful—

something that it would be difficult to miss; they told him that she was accepted in the most elevated of social circles, but that was already clear from the fact that her mother expected a title to accompany her marriage and that she'd already come close to achieving that ambition; they told him that she was twenty-nine, and they also told him, almost as an afterthought, that she was an impressive businesswoman who, with Nick Jefferson, was making serious waves in the growing leisure market.

He wondered briefly how *he* would react if a business profile of him concentrated on his looks and his pedigree and mentioned his achievements almost as an afterthought.

A cool exterior might be one way to handle it. A touch of frost to fool all but the closest observer, as well as to hide a passionate nature and a pair of warm lips.

He pushed the folder away. There was nothing with which to get a hook on the real woman, what made her tick. Nothing to tell him what had driven her to pick up a total stranger on a train and invite him along to her cousin's wedding. Nothing to tell him why she and the belted Earl had called it a day. But he wouldn't find that in the business press. Julie had worked on the only hard facts he had been able to give her and had done her best with them in such a short time. The business press wasn't the place to look; what for, exactly, he couldn't have said, but there *had* to be more.

His door opened and he glanced up. 'Your car is here, Fergus.'

He glanced out of the window as he stood up. A

silver Rolls-Royce was standing at the kerb. 'A Rolls?' he queried.

'It's the only possible car when you're wearing a hat this big,' Julie murmured, repeating his hands-wide-apart gesture. And she picked an infinitesimal piece of fluff from his top hat before handing it to him with the merest suspicion of a smile. 'Have a nice wedding.'

'Nice?' He considered the matter as he took the hat from her. 'The only thing I'm certain of is that it will be interesting.'

'Really? Is there some doubt that the groom will show up?' she asked, following him to the door of his office. 'Or the bride? Or do you have some advance information on the subject of "just cause and impediment"?'

'I couldn't say to the first two questions, since I've never met either of them, Julie, and no to the third.'

'Then it must be Miss Veronica Grant and her large hat who will provide the interest,' she suggested, her eyes sparkling behind the pair of spectacles she had recently taken to wearing. 'Tell me, your club is one of those dreary, old-fashioned, men-only places, isn't it?'

'It is neither dreary, nor old-fashioned. It is a haven of peace and tranquillity where a man can relax safe in the knowledge—'

'As I thought, men only. Are *you* sure you'll be wanting that room?'

'Why wouldn't I?'

'Because Veronica Grant is a lovely-looking woman. And because it's time you stopped worrying about everyone else, Fergus, and started having some fun.'

'Thank you, Julie. I'll bear that in mind.' But he smiled as he headed for the lift, recalling that doorstep kiss. If he was looking for fun, hot ice cream might be a promising place to start.

CHAPTER FIVE

THE Rolls came to halt at Suzie Broughton's front door a minute or two before one-thirty, and when Fergus rang the bell it was answered with such immediacy by Suzie, now wearing an elegant suit and holding a hat the size of a cartwheel, that he suspected she had been lying in wait behind the curtains for him.

'Mr Kavanagh, do come in,' she invited.

'Fergus, please,' he said, depositing his gloves and hat on a small Sheraton table in the hall.

'Fergus,' she repeated obediently. 'And I'm Suzie. Come through into the sitting room. Veronica will be down in a moment. Would you like a drink while you're waiting?'

'No. Thank you.' He had no idea what Veronica had told this woman, but he wasn't fooled for a minute by her easy charm. Her eager eyes gave her away, and he knew that he was in for a grilling. It was certainly not the moment to dull his wits with alcohol.

'Have you known Ronnie long, Fergus?'

'Ronnie? Oh, you mean Veronica.'

'Hmm.' She gave him a thoughtful look. 'Ronnie's been avoiding questions, too. You know, you're both being so cagey that a suspicious mind would think the pair of you had something to hide.'

She wasn't wasting any time getting to the point. Veronica must have kept her very short of information. 'What could I...we...possibly have to hide?' he asked.

'You see? You're doing it again. Answering my question with another question. It's a technique I know well,' she said, with a shameless grin. 'I use it myself all the time, when I don't have the right answers.'

'I can't believe that you're ever short of the right answers, Suzie.'

She continued to smile. 'You're good, Fergus. Very good. That's the trouble.' Fergus assumed what he hoped was a suitably puzzled expression. 'You've both gone to far too much trouble to avoid a question as simple as when you met—'

'Suz!' A man's desperate voice called from above.

'But it seems that you've been saved by Nigel. For now.' She cast an exasperated glance at the ceiling as the call was repeated, rather more loudly. 'He's a love, but absolutely hopeless with shirt-studs. I'll have to go and help him.'

'Please don't let me detain you,' he said, earning himself another, this time appreciative, smile.

'As I said, you're very good, Fergus, but give me time and I'll have all your little secrets. You see if I don't.'

'I'll try and be patient,' he said, returning her smile with interest as a final, infuriated demand for her presence above sent her flying from the room.

Fergus was standing by a pair of open French windows looking down into a small courtyard garden when her scent alerted him to the fact that he was no longer alone. Gardenia. That was the flower that had eluded him. It was the top note of a scent that could have been created just for her. Cool at first, but with an undercurrent of something warm, something unexpected. He turned and she was standing just inside the doorway, quite still, watching him.

She was wearing a heavy silk coat-dress with a small collar that stood away a little from her neck to display the plaited gold necklace that lay about her throat. The dress was a silvery blue that exactly matched her eyes, accentuating the dark, inviting richness of her mouth. Her hair, which this morning had been worn loose in a neat page-boy bob, had been coiled in some simple style on top of her head, and the contents of the troublesome hatbox, little more than a stiffened circle of the same material as her dress, had been pinned in place by a dashing gold hatpin.

She looked absolutely stunning. Breathtaking. At least, she had taken his breath away.

'Do you suppose,' she asked, finally breaking the seemingly endless silence that seemed to stretch between them as she crossed the room to join him by the window, 'that men cease to be able to do the simplest things for themselves the moment they marry?'

'I beg your pardon?'

'Apart from the obvious things, like sending birthday cards to their mothers or making appointments at the dentist. I mean the simple things, like cufflinks, studs, cravats.' She paused. 'Shoelaces, for all I know. You don't have a wife to fuss about you, yet you managed to get here on time, fully dressed. Or does your club have a valet?'

'What?' Then, 'No. At least, I've never… I didn't

go…' He made an effort to pull himself together. 'Is this relevant?'

'Not at all,' she replied solemnly. 'I was just thinking out loud. I like your new suit. So few men have a morning coat that fits them properly.'

He stretched his shoulders and pulled a face. 'I hate wearing new clothes.' He paused. 'You look quite lovely.'

'Thank you.'

'The hat is a real head-turner. Worth all the—' He broke off as Suzie returned, hat in place and apparently eager to be off, although still fiddling impatiently with a troublesome cufflink while Veronica introduced Nigel Broughton. As they shook hands, Veronica raised a conspiratorial eyebrow in his direction. *You see?* she seemed to be saying. And Fergus felt an odd warmth seep through him as she invited him to share her unspoken amusement.

'How are you getting to the church?' he enquired, turning back swiftly to Nigel Broughton in an attempt to cover his intense desire to take her hand, to touch her. Then, conscious of Suzie's eyes on them, he wondered if he *should* take her hand. Or would that look too much as if they were playing a part? Like working too hard at avoiding simple questions. Instead, he said, 'Can we offer you both a lift?'

Nigel opened his mouth, but what his response would have been was lost in Suzie's immediate acceptance. 'How kind. We'll never get a taxi at this time of day.' Her glance at her husband suggested that in failing to provide suitable transport for the occasion he had fallen sadly short of expectations. Nigel did not look in the least bit bothered.

Fergus handed Veronica into the rear of the Rolls and turned to offer the same service to Suzie. But she was still fussing over Nigel's appearance, twitching his cravat into place, and she waved distractedly at him to join Veronica. Finally she gave up attempting to turn Nigel into the modern-day equivalent of Beau Brummell, and allowed herself to be helped into the car alongside Fergus, before her husband took the front seat beside the driver.

Fergus had intended to sit there himself, but now he found himself pressed against Veronica, the cool floral perfection of her scent stealing over him as they pulled out into the King's Road. He glanced at her, and assured, confident, she did not turn away. She was every inch a woman who was in control of her own life, the epitome of the successful modern woman. And yet today she had professed the need of a man on her arm, a man to shield her from a meddling mother.

He had seized the opportunity she had offered without thinking too hard about her motives, which was unlike him. He was not usually given to off-the-cuff decisions. But he should have thought about it, because it was obvious, on reflection, that Veronica Grant was a woman more than capable of handling an interfering mother and any number of unwelcome suitors without raising her pulse-rate by so much as a beat.

Suzie turned at that moment, and, intercepting the look, smiled the way women do when they think they are part of some romantic conspiracy, and for a moment he wondered if Suzie knew. If she was part of this game and had merely been teasing him…

As if somehow she had picked up his thoughts, Veronica gave the slightest shake of her head, a flicker of her long lids that said they were alone in this. Just the two of them. And the corners of her mouth lifted imperceptibly, a tiny crease appearing in the smooth contour of her cheek to underline the secret smile that locked them together in their private pact.

He had to tear his gaze from her mouth, remembering the warmth of her lips as he had surprised her with a kiss, her startled response, the unexpected flare of heat in her silvery eyes. He hadn't been able to stop himself from thinking what it would be like to kiss her when she was waiting for him to kiss her, wanting him to kiss her, what it would be like to drown in melting ice cream…

Suzie's eyes never left them as they drove through the crowded streets, flickering back and forth, storing up each intimate exchange of glances, each small, private smile to relay at the gossipy coffee morning circuit, or at the gym, or while she powdered her nose at a dozen dinner parties. He wondered if Veronica had foreseen that as a complication. Or whether she would welcome this extension to their little charade. Whatever it was.

The car crept forward a few feet at a time, and he glanced at his watch as they edged along Birdcage Walk. 'We should have started out earlier,' he said.

'A water main burst in Victoria Street,' the driver explained. 'But don't worry, the bride is certain to be at least fifteen minutes late.'

'Sure to be,' Nigel agreed. 'Maybe more. Suzie kept me waiting a full twenty minutes.'

'Did she?' Poppy had been unfashionably prompt

when she had married Richard. 'I've never quite understood the reason for that.'

Suzie grinned. 'It doesn't do to appear too eager, Fergus. We can't have you men taking us for granted.'

Somehow he didn't think that Nigel was ever given the chance. 'I'd have thought the altar was a bit late for those kinds of games,' he replied. But it explained about Poppy. She and Richard couldn't wait to be married and didn't care who knew it. Dora and John appeared to feel the same way, and he sincerely hoped that if he ever felt sufficiently moved to ask a woman to marry him she would be every bit as eager. Just so long as the bride was one of his own choosing.

The driver, grinning, caught his eye in the mirror. 'Bachelor, are you, sir?'

About to say 'and planning to stay that way,' Fergus was suddenly aware of Veronica's stillness beside him, an almost tangible silence as the other two occupants of the car awaited his answer. It was time to forget all about Poppy and Dora's plots and start playing his part in earnest.

'For the moment,' he said.

On one side of him Suzie let out a satisfied little sigh. On the other Veronica's hand, resting beside his on the seat between them, briefly touched his, and he turned to her.

From beneath the brim of her hat her eyes seemed huge as she silently mouthed the words 'thank you'.

Any time. The unspoken words filled his head. Anything.

One wedding was very much like another, Fergus thought, if you were a guest. All the men were dressed in clothes designed to make them indistinguishable from one another, and all the women were dressed if not to kill, then certainly to wound with intent.

The bride's appearance wrought a sigh and a flutter of lace-edged handkerchiefs from the female section of the congregation. The page-boys giggled at the bridegroom's middle names as he stuttered nervously over his vows. The older bridesmaids fluttered their lashes at the best man, neglecting to keep their eyes on the little ones who chewed their posies, tugged off their headdresses and had to be captured and corralled by their mothers when they got thoroughly bored with the entire proceedings.

The only difference about this wedding was the glances, the murmurs of interest that it had been impossible to ignore as the usher had shown them into their seat near the back of the church. Veronica clearly hadn't exaggerated the interest that her appearance would provoke, but she had appeared utterly unaware of it as she had slipped quickly along the pew next to Suzie, so that he was standing next to the aisle.

At least the lateness of their arrival had avoided the necessity for endless introductions to these curious strangers, although the surreptitious looks that they continued to attract throughout the service suggested these had simply been put on hold. At any other social occasion it would have been easy to miss, but it was difficult to be surreptitious in a hat the size of a cartwheel, and cartwheels seemed to be in the majority.

Fergus was an intensely private man. He'd never been given to public handholding, or any of those other faintly embarrassing displays of affection lovers seemed to indulge in. Perhaps that was the reason his sisters assumed he would be grateful for their assistance in finding him a wife.

But it was one thing keeping emotions firmly under wraps when there were impressionable teenagers around to giggle and tease a big brother who had trouble enough keeping them in line; there was no necessity for it here.

So, while the hats turned in unison to witness the arrival of the bride, and didn't waste the opportunity to see who Veronica had brought to Fliss's wedding, he took her hand in his. She glanced up at him, momentarily startled by the unexpected contact, then realising what he was doing, she smiled and left her hand in his as she watched the bride moving slowly up the aisle on her father's arm.

Then she sighed a little. 'Such a pretty girl,' she murmured, retrieving her hand and flipping open the service sheet.

'Yes,' he agreed, although, if he was quite honest, he had scarcely noticed the bride.

'Everyone into line, please.' The photographer was not to be denied. He wanted a group shot and he wanted it now. 'Cuddle up nice and close and smile, everyone. This is a wedding...'

Fergus put his arm about Veronica's shoulders and eased her slightly in front of him, holding her close as they bunched up tightly. 'Is your mother here?' he murmured.

'She's here.' Her mother had been bearing down on them when she had been corralled into the photograph, but that wouldn't hold her for long. 'Don't worry, she'll have spotted you.'

'Smile everyone, please.' They smiled obediently.

'Are you quite sure you're ready for this, Fergus?' She turned to look up at him. 'We could make a run for it; it's not too late.'

'Once more, please. Big smile, everyone.'

'I'm not scared of your mother,' he said, as they turned once more to face the camera.

'Many a foolish word—' she began, as the group quickly broke up. She didn't have time to finish.

'*There* you are, Veronica,' her mother declared. 'You were so late, I was beginning to think you weren't coming.' But it was Fergus who took the full force of her personality as she stared at him, absorbing every detail, including the fact that he had his arm around her daughter, that they were standing very close and were apparently smiling at some little secret.

'The traffic was terrible,' Veronica said, bending obediently to make a sketch at a kiss. 'We had to slip in at the back. Mother, may I introduce Fergus Kavanagh?' And she turned to Fergus. 'Fergus, this is my mother. Annette Grant.'

Fergus extended his right hand, keeping Veronica's shoulder firmly grasped in his left. He'd been asked to convince this woman, and anyone else who was interested, that they were lovers. It was his pleasure. 'How d'you do, Mrs Grant?'

Annette Grant took his hand, her forehead puckered in concentration. 'Kavanagh? I've heard that name somewhere recently—'

'Have you?' he enquired. 'Well, I'm sure it's common enough.'

'Where was it, now?'

'Mother—' Veronica attempted to distract her '—I think we should be leaving.'

'Are you related to *Dora* Kavanagh, by any chance?'

Veronica could scarcely believe her ears. Her mother *knew* Dora Kavanagh? Why ever had she thought this was going to be simple? But Fergus didn't appear in the least bit concerned. 'She's my younger sister,' he confirmed, with the kind of smile that she knew would have her mother eating out of his hand. She rather thought he knew it too.

And indeed, Annette Grant's face relaxed into a smile. 'Well, that's it. She was giving a talk at a fund-raiser for refugees a few weeks ago. She's a fine girl. You must be proud of her.'

'So she keeps telling me,' Fergus replied.

Mrs Grant turned to the young man at her side. 'Go and see if our car is in sight, Gerry,' she said, dismissing him. 'I think the bride's about to leave.'

'But—'

But it was obvious that Gerry was now surplus to requirements. Annette Grant was far more interested in her daughter's companion. 'She's getting married shortly, isn't she?' she said, giving Veronica what could only be described as a pointed look.

'Dora? Yes, in a couple of weeks,' he replied. 'Veronica has promised to come down for the wedding.' He glanced down at her. 'Haven't you, darling?'

She began to relax. Fergus felt the tension easing from her shoulder, saw the sparkle return to her eyes as the moment passed. 'I wouldn't miss it for the world,' she replied.

'Really?' Annette Grant's expression took on a

more speculative cast. 'And is that how you met Veronica? Through Dora?'

'Through Dora?' Then, 'Oh, no. We met quite by chance. On a train.'

'Over the *Financial Times*,' Veronica added. Then, provokingly, 'It's such a romantic shade of pink, don't you think?'

'Don't be flippant, Veronica.' Annette Grant continued to address her remarks to Fergus. 'On a train, you say? When was this?'

Maybe not quite the 'third degree', Fergus decided, but getting close. 'We were coming up to town, and somehow ended up at the same table for breakfast.' Nothing but the truth. But not exactly what Annette Grant wanted to know.

Before she could press the point, however, Veronica said, 'Fergus is a kipper man, Mother.' She turned to him and added confidentially, 'My father adored kippers, too.'

'Really?'

'He always had them when he breakfasted on the train. Mother wouldn't allow them at home,' Veronica continued. Her face was straight enough, but her eyes were sparkling with mischief as she wound her mother up.

'Well.' For the moment Annette Grant seemed lost for words. 'Well, the smell does *linger* so...'

'It does,' Fergus agreed, and Annette Grant gave her daughter a look that said, *You see?* 'Perhaps I could offer you both a lift to the reception?' she suggested as the bride and groom finally prepared to leave. Then, irritably, 'What *is* it, Gerry?'

'Rose petals,' he said, offering her a small bag stuffed with them. 'You said you wanted rose petals.'

'Did I?' Annette Grant gave the impression that she had never heard the words 'rose' or 'petal' before.

'Fresh ones. You insisted. I picked them for you this morning. You left them in the car.'

'If you say so, Gerry.' She took the bag and peered inside. 'They're going brown at the edges,' she complained. Then, seeing Gerry's face, said more kindly, 'Never mind. I don't suppose Fliss will notice. Come along, Veronica, let's go and strew the bride's path.'

'But...' Then she threw a hopeless grin at Fergus, a look that said, *See? I wasn't exaggerating, was I?*

And he did see. Veronica hadn't exaggerated about Annette Grant. Formidable with a capital F. Although if she was planning to tempt her daughter into matrimony she would have to do a lot better than Gerry.

'We'll catch up with you at the reception, Mrs Grant,' he said, his hand clamped firmly on Veronica's shoulder. 'I know you'll excuse us the rose petals.'

For a moment he thought she was going to argue. Her mouth opened slightly. But then it closed again. 'Yes. Yes, of course. Do run along. We'll talk later.' It sounded more like a threat than a promise. 'Come along, Gerry.'

Veronica watched in astonishment as her mother joined the crowd gathering about the bridal car. 'Amazing,' she said. 'If I hadn't seen it with my own eyes...'

He grinned. 'You didn't choose me just because of my good looks, did you? Come on, let's get out of here.'

'But what about Suzie and Nigel?'

'They'll find us.' And without waiting for her response he took her elbow and led the way through the gate, up the road to where the Rolls was waiting.

The driver had seen them coming, and had opened the door for them, but Veronica stopped a little way short of the car. 'Fergus…'

'Yes?'

She lifted her face to his, tilting back her head a little so that her hat did not cover her eyes. 'I just…that is…I wanted to say…' She gave the tiniest of shrugs. 'Thank you. That's all.'

He lifted his hand to her cheek and for a moment they stood there, sightseers, wedding guests, civil servants streaming past them.

'Veronica!' Suzie hurried up to them, clutching at her hat. 'Oh, thank goodness,' she said. 'I thought you'd left without us.'

Fergus held Veronica's gaze locked in his for seconds longer, and for just a moment he put his own hand on hers where it lay on his sleeve. Then he turned to Suzie, switching on a smile as he did so. 'You didn't think we'd leave without you, surely?' he asked.

'It was a bit of a crush at the church,' Veronica said quickly. 'We thought we'd wait here for you.'

'Oh, don't apologise. I wouldn't have blamed you if you *had* gone. Nigel can never stop talking.' She turned to Veronica. 'Wasn't it the most gorgeous wedding? And Fliss was wearing the Carteret tiara, did you see? Not that it compares with the Glendale diamonds—' She stopped, horrified at what she'd said.

'You were at George's wedding?' Veronica asked

without expression, without showing the slightest emotion. She'd had a lot of practice at that.

'He's a distant cousin of Nigel's,' Suzie said awkwardly. 'Oh, thank goodness. Here he is at last. I'm absolutely desperate for champagne. There's nothing like hymns about abiding love to dry the throat.'

Or opening your mouth and putting your foot in it, Fergus thought.

The mirrored ballroom of the hotel reception suite sparkled with huge Viennese chandeliers, and the famous Carteret tiara reflected endlessly as the bride and groom lined up with their immediate families to receive their guests, all kisses and smiles.

'Fliss, darling,' Veronica said, kissing the air a centimetre from her cheek. 'You look like a princess. Every happiness.' Then she turned to introduce Fergus. 'May I introduce—?'

But Fliss was smiling broadly as she offered her hand. 'Introductions aren't necessary. Fergus and I have met before.'

'Have we?' Fergus stared at the vibrant young woman. 'Are you sure? I can't believe that I could possibly have forgotten anyone quite so lovely.'

Fliss laughed. 'Don't worry, you aren't losing your memory. I was rising thirteen at the time, a spotty adolescent with braces. I was at school with Dora,' she explained. 'You took us both out to tea when you came down for Open Day.'

'Did I? And you remembered?'

'It was a very good tea,' she said. 'And there was the added fun that afterwards the entire sixth form were given detention for wearing lipstick on your account.'

'But that's terrible.' Veronica raised a querying eyebrow a fraction of an inch in his direction. 'They went to all that trouble and I didn't even notice,' he said. The eyebrow was hitched a disbelieving millimetre higher.

'I did invite Dora today,' Fliss said, still laughing. 'But with her own wedding so close...'

Now that would have been interesting. 'It's true that she's up to her eyes in planning last-minute details,' he confirmed. But relief came a moment too soon.

'She said she'd drop in later if she could get away.'

'I had no idea.' He caught Veronica's eye. 'It's highly unusual for our social calendars to collide.'

'I'm so sorry that I'll be away for her wedding,' Fliss said.

'I'm quite sure she understands that your honeymoon must come before such pleasures,' he sympathised gravely. 'But Veronica will be there. She'll make an excellent deputy.'

The new Lady Carteret laughed at that. 'Ronnie's never been anyone's deputy, Fergus. She's always been number one.'

'Not in this relationship.' He was well aware that Annette Grant was standing a few feet from them. 'We share top billing.'

Fliss beamed. 'How absolutely perfect,' she declared.

'We think so.'

They moved on, and he took two glasses of champagne from a passing waiter, handing one to

Veronica. 'The *entire* sixth form?' she enquired finally. 'All those pouting seventeen-year-olds and you expect me to believe that you didn't notice?'

'Believe it,' he said. 'I worked very hard at not noticing; there is no more dangerous combination than gym slips and lipstick. Besides, the headmistress wanted a donation for the new science block, so she used it as an excuse to whisk me away for a glass of sherry.'

'Did she get her donation?'

'Rather more easily than she expected, I suspect. I was desperate to escape. I sent Poppy in my place the following year.'

'Spoilsport.'

But she didn't have a chance to tease him further before they were inundated with friends who hadn't seen Veronica for months and who clearly wanted to catch up on her life. And her new man.

He shook hands, smiled politely, and found to his relief that the men were more interested in his views on the stockmarket than in how long he had known Veronica.

'Annette tells me that you met in the rain,' one elderly dowager said, rather loudly, during a lull. 'Taking shelter, were you?'

'No, Aunt May, we met on a train,' Veronica said, stooping to speak clearly into the old lady's ear.

'Dratted thing,' she said, fiddling with her hearing aid. Then, 'You should never shelter under trees, you know. Dangerous things, trees. Especially elms.'

'There aren't many elms left,' Fergus pointed out. 'We had to fell dozens in the park—'

'And a good thing, too. Treacherous things, elms.

The branch of one missed me by inches once. I'd crept out to spoon with Bertie in the woods when I should have been in bed, and it just dropped, without warning. They do that, you know. It could have killed me.' Then she chuckled. 'That would have left Bertie with some explaining to do, eh!'

'You see, Ronnie?' Suzie said with a knowing smile. 'I told you trees were nasty, dangerous things.' She helped herself to another glass of champagne from a passing waiter. 'So, tell me about this tree you met under.'

'May's the expert on trees,' Veronica reminded her. 'Why don't you ask her about it?'

Suzie merely sipped her drink and looked smug. 'Never mind, I'll get to the bottom of it before the day's over.'

'There's nothing to get to the bottom of. I told you, we met on a train.'

'Over breakfast. I remember.'

'Then we met again by chance,' Fergus intervened and glanced at Veronica, leaving her to fill in the details. Just in case she had already said something.

'At the museum,' she obliged.

'The museum! Oh, come on, Ronnie! Even in Melchester you must have better things to do than hang around museums.'

'It was a cocktail party,' Fergus pointed out. 'We know how to enjoy ourselves in Melchester. Even in museums.' Having been given a lead, he was quite capable of improvising. 'It was for the opening of the new Kavanagh Room, Suzie. There's a display of the most interesting potsherds. You must see it when you come down to visit Veronica.' Veronica was avoiding his eye, Fergus thought, because she was trying very hard not to laugh. He thought he would enjoy seeing her laugh.

'What the devil are potsherds?' Suzie demanded.

'Bits of pot,' Veronica said, taking up the story. 'They were dug up by Fergus's mother. You remember, Suzie, when you were showing off your perfect recall this morning, you mentioned that Mrs Kavanagh was an archaeologist?'

'So I did.' Suzie was looking at them like a woman who knows she's having her leg pulled, but can't quite put her finger on how.

'Then we saw one another again at a concert.' Fergus steered the inquisition smoothly on, before Suzie started to ask questions that might leave Veronica floundering.

'Bumping into one another was getting to be quite a habit, then?'

'Melchester is a small city.'

'Even so.'

'Even so,' Fergus agreed, 'our tastes do seem to have a pleasurable synchronicity.' Veronica gazed at the chandeliers, biting on her lower lip. Suzie simply stared at him. 'And when, in the course of conversation, we discovered that we both had tickets for a new play… What was it, now, Veronica? Something by Oscar Wilde…'

'An Ideal Husband,' she said quickly.

'Of course. *An Ideal Husband.* It's on a pre-London tour. Worth seeing, wouldn't you say?' He glanced at Veronica. Any minute now and she would lose control. He rather relished the idea of seeing her throw back her head and laugh out loud at something he had said.

But she cleared her throat, straightened her face. 'Definitely worth seeing,' she agreed.

'Anyway, when we discovered we had tickets for the same play, we decided it was time to start caring for the environment.' Suzie continued to stare at him. 'Stop wasting petrol and use one car,' he explained.

'Very laudable. But you know the logical extension to that argument, don't you?' They waited, well aware that they were about to be enlightened. 'Double up on everything,' she continued. 'Including the bed.'

'Really? I hadn't thought of that.' He turned to Veronica, his face straight. 'Had you thought of that, Veronica?'

She looked thoughtful. 'No. That one slipped by me. Worth considering, though.'

'Oh, sure,' Suzie said, unconvinced, as she was meant to be.

'What was that you said about leaving early?' he asked, as the swell of guests moved on and for a moment they were alone. 'Your friend Suzie has promised me the third degree. So far she's barely reached the second, and your mother was cut short at the church, but somehow I fancy Dora will be a lot harder to fool.' Her eyes were sparkling with amusement. 'It's not funny, Veronica. You won't be able to distract my little sister with a kipper.'

'I won't need a kipper. Keep this up and we'll have people asking when we're going to set the date for our own wedding.'

'What a pity I didn't think to get a ring. If we

pretended to be engaged, no one would bother us for years.'

'It would be a little sudden, don't you think?'

'Not if you're a Kavanagh,' he assured her. 'We're known for the suddenness of our attachments.'

'So I've heard. I'd better warn you, Suzie already knows a great deal about you.'

'I rather thought she might be a gossip queen.'

'And we'd have to be seen together on a regular basis.'

'I wouldn't consider that a hardship.'

'No,' she said. 'Neither would I.' And then she blushed. 'But perhaps we should keep that as a contingency plan for the future.' There was going to be a future, then? He was tempted to ask her, but she was regarding him from beneath her lashes in a manner that drove everything else from his mind. 'If we announce it now, everyone will get excited and expect us to set a date for the wedding—'

'Date for the wedding?' Lady May, who had been standing several feet away, making her way through a tray full of canapés while she continued to twiddle with her hearing aid, suddenly beamed at them. 'It's working,' she said, as they turned at her loud exclamation. 'Annette didn't tell me that you're getting married, Veronica.' Her voice had the cut-glass carrying power of a stage duchess, and the loud buzz of conversation died as she complained, 'But then nobody ever tells me anything.'

CHAPTER SIX

INTO the sudden silence, when Annette Grant, along with most of those present, turned as one to look at them, the sounding of a gong and the solemn announcement that they should take their places for luncheon came as a welcome relief.

For a moment it had looked as if Veronica's mother was about to confront them, but she'd clearly thought better of it, and instead turned to her companion with a distant smile, as if this were something she wasn't ready to talk about. But it was simply a breathing space. They both knew it.

'Well,' Fergus said, as the noise of conversation swelled louder than ever as the guests sought their seats. 'That should give everyone something to talk about over lunch.'

'Fergus, I'm so—'

'Just remember, Veronica,' he said gravely, before she could apologise. 'Absolutely no balloons.'

'Balloons?' She stared at him for a moment. 'This is not funny—'

He smiled anyway. 'Oh, I don't know. It does have a certain entertainment value. And just think how much worse it could have been.'

'Worse?' she began, then realising that several people had turned as her voice rose, she stopped. Gathered herself. 'How?' she demanded through clenched teeth.

'I could have been the fake Italian count.' For a moment she stared at him. 'Or Gerry.'

'Fergus, this is no joking matter—'

'Then why are you laughing?'

'I'm not,' she protested. But she was. She was trying very hard not to, but he could see it there, in her eyes. In the tiny creases at the corners of her mouth. Trying to get out. She was having to work very hard not to let it.

'Come on, let's face the music. We're on table three,' he said. '"Miss Veronica Grant and partner". Tell me,' he asked, keeping her talking as they crossed the room, so that she wouldn't be quite so conscious of the ripple of interest that followed their progress, 'what would you have done if I hadn't co-operated in this little charade?'

She grabbed at the welcome change of subject. 'I was working on my excuse for the non-appearance of "and partner" when I saw you get on the train,' she confessed.

'Some urgent business meeting, no doubt?'

'Absolutely vital to the stability of international trade.'

'New York?'

'Too close. Three hours by Concorde. Hardly any excuse at all.'

'Hong Kong, then?'

'Safer.'

'But not so much fun.'

She wasn't certain about fun. All she knew was that this "little charade" was becoming more dangerous by the minute. 'This is certainly more exciting,' she admitted.

Good choice of words. He hadn't been so excited about anything or anyone for a long time. 'But convincing, do you think?'

'You've certainly convinced Aunt May. And just about everyone here.'

'Including Suzie?'

'Ah, Suzie…' And she finally let loose the laughter that she had been holding back, a silvery ripple of sound that made heads turn. It made his heart leap to hear it. 'Suzie is totally convinced that we're lovers—your kiss did that.'

'Well, that's good. Isn't it?'

Oh, yes, it was good. Very good. Two unattached people hell-bent on avoiding matrimony might have a lot of fun, she thought. 'And Aunt May has just answered any question she might have been saving up.'

'Except the date,' Fergus reminded her. 'But we can leave your mother to sort that one out over lunch.' He tucked her arm beneath his. 'Meanwhile, we can enjoy ourselves. Let's go and find our table before Lady May turns her hearing aid on us again.'

He pulled back a chair for her and she sat down, introducing him to those guests he had not already met. The food arrived, the wine was excellent, and everyone tactfully avoided any mention of their future plans. Instead, he listened to the woman on his right, who was keen to talk about Dora's charity work, acknowledged an acquaintance from some Mansion House dinner, and discussed the chances of one of his horses winning at Newmarket the following week with a woman who clearly knew her stuff.

Then he looked up and saw that Annette Grant was

regarding her daughter, a small frown creasing her well-preserved brow. She wasn't quite convinced, he sensed. It was all too sudden. Too unlikely that her career-minded daughter would suddenly go weak at the knees for romance. Well, he'd just have to try harder to convince the lady. He slid his arm along the back of Veronica's chair and leaned closer.

'Where are all these suitors I'm supposed to be fending off?' he murmured as she turned to him.

'Your presence is enough to keep them at bay, and Aunt May's public announcement of our forthcoming nuptials should finish the job. Maybe I should take you up on that offer of a long-term engagement.' She'd spoken without thinking, he knew. But now they were both thinking, and for a moment they were silent in the face of the possibilities conjured up across the wedding favours and the wreckage of the lunch table.

Then the bride's father rose to his feet and Veronica turned to listen. Fergus didn't hear him, or the bridegroom or the best man. Instead, he simply took pleasure in watching Veronica, enjoying the purity of her profile, the sudden laughter that fanned the delicate skin around her eyes, the appearance of an unexpected dimple at the corner of her mouth. A permanent engagement. Now there was a thought.

Then the newly-weds took to the floor to begin the dancing and Annette Grant rose too. But not to dance. She had waited all through a very long lunch for answers, and now she was going to get them. But not yet, he thought, as she made her way slowly through the ballroom, constantly stopped by friends who were no doubt eager to congratulate her, eager for details. Not yet.

'Are you ready for that dance, Veronica?' he asked her.

'*Can* you dance?' she asked.

'I doubt if I can compete with the Italian count, but I think I can manage to steer you gently around the ballroom without stepping on your toes. Once around the floor and then a quick dash for the exit, I think you said.'

She laughed, as he had hoped she would. 'After Aunt May's announcement, the quicker the better. But you're right, not before we've danced just once, so that everyone can have a good look at you.'

'In that case, let's ditch the hat.'

'Oh, yes…' She reached for the pin, but he forestalled her.

'Here, let me do that.' And he leaned across her and removed the pin, before lifting the hat clear of her head. 'You shouldn't ever cover your hair,' he said, tucking a delicate strand of platinum-pale hair back into place. A small, possessive gesture; he could almost feel Annette Grant's frustration as she was delayed by friends.

They would have to own up soon enough, but for now, in the eyes of the world, the lady was his and he planned to make the most of it. He stood up and, dropping her hat onto his chair, took her hand and clasped it as she rose to her feet, leading her to the dance floor where he eased her gently into his arms, holding her for a moment before they began to move slowly in time to the music.

Holding her, he discovered, put every one of his

senses on overtime. Her hair, just below the level of his eyes, shone like white gold. Her scent was faint, elusive. He'd once read that dancing was the vertical expression of a horizontal desire, and now the touch of her skin as her slender hand lay in his, the silk-covered movement of her body beneath his palm, sparked just that kind of response in him. In that moment he ached to possess her as she had, in a few short hours, somehow come to possess him.

And when she lifted her head and smiled up at him he found he could recall the taste of her mouth, warm and honeyed and full of a promise all the sweeter for being unexpected. He finally understood the instant attraction that had fired both Poppy and Dora when they had encountered the men in their life. The way Poppy had defied convention to move in with Richard the day they had met… The way Dora had risked everything for John…

There had been no uncertainty, no soul-searching for them. They had known. He knew. Just as he knew it would be a mistake to say anything, do anything.

His sisters had fallen instantly in love with men who had responded with equal fervour. He sensed that Veronica, confident and mature as she was in her professional life, would find it hard to surrender to the unreasoning power of love at first sight, would find it difficult to trust emotion over logic. And he wondered how much of that diffidence could be laid at the feet of George Glendale, now apparently married to someone else.

'Say something,' he said, his own voice huskier than he remembered.

She looked up at him. 'What?'

'It doesn't matter. I just wanted to hear your voice.'

'Fergus...'

'That's nice, too.' But Veronica had stopped dancing, and as he looked up he could see why.

'Is this true?' Annette Grant, dancing with the hapless Gerry, had manoeuvred her way towards them and now blocked them. Her face was smiling benevolently at them, but her voice, low though it was, was tight with anger.

It was not a moment for hesitation; it was time to act, and Fergus did just that. With one arm around Veronica's shoulders and one around her mother's, he eased them both towards the tropical water garden. 'Why don't we all go and have a drink?' he suggested. 'You will excuse us, Gerry?' The man disappeared with grateful alacrity.

'Mother,' Veronica began soothingly as they left the ballroom, 'I can explain.'

But her mother was in no mood to be soothed. 'Have you any idea what I've been through in the last two hours? The congratulations, the questions? Questions, I might add, to which I have no answers—'

'A bottle of Bolly, I think,' he said, before Veronica could offer any. She threw him a startled glance as her mother sank on to one of the elegant wooden seats beside the waterfall. 'Veronica, I wonder, would you like to check if Dora has turned up?'

Veronica stared at him. 'Dora?' She had never met Dora, had no idea what Dora looked like.

'Maybe she would like to join us.'

And then she saw that he was giving her a chance to escape for a few minutes so that she wouldn't have to face her mother alone while he organised the champagne.

'Oh, yes. What a good idea. Will you excuse me, Mother?' And she turned quickly and walked away before her mother could object.

'Young man.' The deaf dowager cut Fergus off as he headed for the bar.

'Lady May. What can I do for you?'

'May, dear, just call me May,' she said. 'And you can get me a drink—a proper drink, none of that fizzy rubbish.'

'Of course. What would you like?'

'A large Scotch. No water, no ice.'

He nodded to the barman. 'And a bottle of Bollinger, please.'

'Yes, sir. I'll bring them over.'

'I'll have mine here.' The old lady eased herself onto a bar stool. 'I loathe weddings, don't you?' she said. 'Nothing but gossipy women in big hats speculating on how long it'll last, wimpy men in fancy dress and fizzy muck to drink.'

May, he realised, got her kicks from shocking people. 'They keep the catering industry in work,' he replied.

'And divorce lawyers.' Then she snorted. 'And milliners. If it hadn't been for weddings and Ascot, they'd have gone out of business years ago.' She picked up her glass and raised it to him. 'Talking of Ascot, I put a hundred pounds on that horse of yours that won the Gold Cup last year.'

'That was taking a risk. It was an outside chance at best.'

'You weren't there, were you? At Ascot.'

'No, unfortunately. I was in the States on business.'

'You have to get your priorities right, young man. Business never goes away—a Gold Cup winner comes along once in a lifetime.' She sipped her whisky and looked at him with a pair of shrewd, button-bright eyes. 'So does the right woman. Sometimes,' she added, 'when you least expect it.'

He regarded her thoughtfully. 'Tell me, May, just how much of our conversation *did* you overhear?'

'Enough.' And she chuckled as she tapped her hearing aid. 'My daughter wants me to get a new one of these, but I get by very nicely with this one. Considering it's so unreliable.'

'If that's so, why did you decide to announce to the gathered assembly that Veronica and I are about to be wed?'

'Because Veronica is a perfectionist. She doesn't believe it's possible to be a successful career woman and a perfect wife... At least that's what she'd have everyone believe.'

'But you don't? Believe it?'

'What I believe is of no interest to anyone these days. What I know, however, is that perfection is the province of God. Mere mortals have to make the best of what comes along. Which is why you're going to get me another drink and then go and make Annette's day.'

'Am I? It won't be easy.'

'Nothing worthwhile ever is.'

'Veronica—'

'Veronica is too controlled for her own good. She

wasn't always like that, and just for a moment, when you made her laugh, I remembered how she used to be.'

Veronica stared at her reflection. What a mess. It was all very well for Fergus to make jokes about balloons, buy champagne, tell her that he'd deal with her mother. Didn't he realise that this was serious?

Two women further down the cloakroom had stopped gossiping and were looking at her. Their faces were vaguely familiar, so she smiled distantly and took out her compact to inspect her nose. Not exactly shiny, but she gave it the powder puff treatment anyway. She might be taking a few moments to gather her wits, but she didn't have to let the whole world know that.

She found her lipstick and freshened the colour on her lips. Maybe she should have taken Fergus up on his offer of a permanent engagement after all... An attractive bachelor on call, one with no desire for marriage, would suit her down to the ground, but it was hardly fair. She snapped her compact shut and put it in her bag. It was time to stop daydreaming and face the music

'Didn't you find Dora?' Fergus asked as she joined him as he walked back to the seat by the waterfall.

She glanced up at him. 'Actually, I didn't look. Was I meant to?'

'No. I just thought you needed a breathing space.' The champagne was waiting at the table for them, a waiter ready to open it. Fergus nodded and the man began to loosen the wire. 'I'm sorry to leave you for so long, Mrs Grant. Lady May buttonholed me at the bar and kept me talking.'

'That woman and her hearing aid. It's all an act, you know.'

'Oh, come on, Mother,' Veronica said, joining her mother on the bench. 'You know you love her to bits.'

'She's a stirrer and a troublemaker and she drinks too much.'

'I know. But she's never dull.'

'That's true.' Annette Grant's face softened a little. 'She certainly livened up lunch. There was only one topic of conversation: when are you two going to set the date for the wedding?'

'Really? How extraordinary. No one even mentioned it at our table.' Fergus glanced at Veronica. 'Did they, darling?'

Veronica's eyes widened momentarily in surprise at the casual endearment. 'No one,' she confirmed.

'It is true, then?'

There are moments, special moments, when a split-second decision will change everything, for always. Veronica had faced one that morning, seizing her moment as he had run for the train. Now it was his turn, and as the champagne cork popped from the bottle and the wine spilled over into the glasses, he picked up one of them and handed it to Annette Grant before lifting his own in silent salute to Veronica.

It was all the answer she needed. 'Darlings! This is wonderful... I don't know what to say...'

'Say nothing,' he advised. And he wasn't talking to Annette Grant.

'But...' Veronica began, then stopped, totally confused, and he handed her the third glass before turning to Annette.

'Just wish us happy.'

'Of course. I couldn't be more pleased. To be honest, I was beginning to think I'd never see the day.'

'Thank you, Mrs Grant.'

'Annette, please. How long have you known?'

'From the moment we first met,' Fergus said.

'Really? Love at first sight? How romantic. You do realise that it'll take at least six months to organise everything properly—' Then, looking and rising quickly to her feet, 'Dora, my dear. Isn't this just the most wonderful news? How long have you known?'

Fergus rose and turned as his sister crossed the acre of carpet and stopped a yard from him, her face racked with disbelief. 'Fergus? Fliss told me...but I could hardly believe it...' But she was clearly determined upon enlightenment. She took a step forward and hugged him, turned to Veronica. 'Won't you introduce us?'

'Veronica, may I introduce my sister, Dora? Dora, Miss Veronica Grant. You already know her mother, I believe.'

'You could have knocked me down with a feather, Dora,' Annette Grant said quickly. 'I had no idea Veronica even knew your brother.'

'Fergus has been very discreet, too,' Dora said, in a 'wait until I get you home' voice. 'Does Poppy know?'

'No one knows,' he said. 'At least, no one knew until today.'

'My husband's old aunt overheard them and gave the game away,' Annette said. 'I couldn't be more pleased.'

'You're pleased too, Dora, aren't you?'

Dora seemed momentarily lost for words. Then her

face relaxed into a smile. 'I couldn't be more delighted, Gussie. Honestly.' And she gave him a big hug. 'Poppy and I have been so worried about who will look after you once I'm married.'

'Really?'

'There we were, racking our brains to think who would make you the perfect wife...'

Veronica was looking up at him, her mouth, her eyes firmly under control. Except for those silver sparks that presaged laughter. 'And had you thought of anyone?' she asked, a dimple appearing unexpectedly at the corner of her mouth.

'It was impossible. Hopeless.'

Fergus cleared his throat warningly. Veronica ignored him. 'Is he so difficult, then?'

'Difficult?' Dora regarded her brother thoughtfully. 'We simply couldn't think of anyone perfect enough—' Fergus turned away as he was apparently caught by a fit of coughing '—but it seems we were worrying needlessly. How did you meet?' she asked.

'Oh, well, Fergus and I have a great many mutual interests,' Veronica replied. 'A dislike of balloons, for instance.'

'Balloons?' Dora repeated as if she couldn't quite trust her ears. Fergus wasn't entirely sure that he believed his own.

'And marquees,' she continued, as if she was genuinely trying to explain the attraction between them. 'Both Fergus and I agree that they are the absolute ruination of a good lawn.' She tilted her head a little and raised her brows a millimetre, inviting him to continue.

Anything to oblige a lady. 'You've forgotten bridesmaids,' he prompted her.

'Bridesmaids?' She appeared to consider the matter for just a moment before she said, 'No. I'm sorry, but we'll have to disagree on the bridesmaids issue, Fergus. A bridesmaid is an absolute necessity.'

'Really?' His surprise was genuine enough.

'Of course. The groom has the best man to take care of the ring. The bride has to have someone to hold her bouquet,' she replied, as if they were quite alone, then added as an afterthought, 'And of course to flirt with the best man.'

'You need at least two, then?'

'Two? Oh, you mean one to take the bouquet and one to flirt?' She appeared to consider it, then shook her head. 'Let's not get carried away, Fergus. I'm sure any reasonably bright girl could manage both.'

'Veronica?' Annette Grant looked momentarily confused, and then she didn't. 'Is this your way of telling me that you're not going to have a big wedding?'

Veronica glanced at Fergus, clearly seeking some clue as to how far he was prepared to go with this nonsense. Another minute of this and they would have set the date and be issuing invitations.

'I thought I might spend the money on buying Veronica a castle instead. Just a little castle,' he replied. *All the way, it seemed. She had no problems with that. Of course, it could just be the champagne thinking, and she'd be sorry in the morning. But they were in too deep now to turn back.* 'One with battlements and a little turret—'

'What on earth would I do with a turret?'

'You're a clever woman. I'm quite sure you could think of something. Would you require a moat?'

'There has to be a moat. With swans.'

'If that's what will make you happy.'

'Except, won't it be damp?' She was trying very hard not to laugh, but she was having a hard time.

'I'll install central heating for you. Maybe we could heat the moat, too, and swim in it—'

She was unable to suppress her laughter a moment longer; it rippled from her so that the nearest guests turned to look in her direction.

'Don't be ridiculous, Fergus.' Annette Grant's voice brought them back to earth.

'Ridiculous?'

'I shall pay for the wedding. Veronica's father left a fund for precisely that purpose.'

'He didn't!'

'Of course he did, Veronica. Your father thought of everything. So buy your castle, Fergus, or whatever other nonsense takes your fancy, and leave the wedding to me. Have you any idea of a date? I believe I did say it will take at least six months to organise properly...' she glanced at Dora '...I'm sure your sister will bear me out on that.'

'But—'

'Six months, minimum,' Dora agreed before he could protest. 'I'm still fiddling about with last-minute details and my wedding is barely two weeks away.'

Fergus smiled at his sister. 'You'll still be making up your mind about those balloons the day before the wedding.'

Dora grinned. 'So many colours, so little time.'

'And I wasn't going to disagree with you. I'm sure

that six months is hardly enough time to organise the kind of wedding that Veronica deserves. I was simply wondering how on earth I can wait that long.'

'For heaven's sake, Fergus,' Veronica said, as they finally made their way to the car. 'We must be sensible. We can't let this go on. After all, we're going to have to own up eventually.'

'Are we?' He grinned, overtaken by a sudden lightness of spirits. 'I don't see why. In fact, I'm beginning to think being sensible is highly overrated.'

'Oh, I stopped being sensible the moment I got on the eight-fifteen this morning. Correction. The moment *you* got on the eight-fifteen this morning.'

'Maybe. But what about our conspiracy?'

'Conspiracy?'

'To remain unwed, despite all the best attempts of our relations.'

'Remain unwed, yes. But you seem to forget that we've set the date,' she exclaimed, 'and we've invited half London to a wedding that isn't going to take place.'

'Things did get a little out of hand,' he agreed. Then grinned and leaned back against the soft leather. 'Perhaps we should have stuck to mineral water.'

'Perhaps!'

'It was a great party, though.'

'Oh, it was a great party. People will be talking about it for months. That's the trouble. What on earth are we going to do, Fergus?'

'Nothing.' He took her hand, held it between his. Then he lifted his arm so that she could lean against him. 'Nothing at all.'

'But the whole point was to *avoid* getting married,' she pointed out, yawning as the champagne combined with the gentle movement of the car to rock her gently towards sleep. 'I have absolutely no intention of getting married, ever. You do understand?'

'Yes, I understand.' He put his arm about her and encouraged her head on to his shoulder. 'And it's not a problem.'

'Isn't it?'

'No.' He was reassuring. He was good at reassuring edgy directors, difficult horses. With luck, he could reassure Veronica. 'We'll simply discover that we're both far too busy to marry in November.'

'It's that simple?' Then, 'Of course. Why didn't I think of that? The months before Christmas are a madhouse. It must have been the champagne, or I'd have realised immediately how impossible it will be.'

'And then there's the problem of Christmas itself,' he reminded her. 'Poppy was married at Christmas. It rained and it was cold. Not that she noticed...but really...no...'

'It would avoid the possibility of a marquee on the lawn,' she pointed out.

'That's true. But if I don't marry at Marlowe Court, the village will miss out on the fun.'

She turned to look up at him. 'What happened to the two witnesses and a register office?'

'Just wishful thinking, I'm afraid. *Noblesse oblige* and all that.' And a sudden understanding of why a wedding should be such a special celebration, why it was important that everyone you knew, cared about, should be there...

She yawned. 'So that would mean spring at the earliest?'

Fergus smiled down at her. 'The very earliest. Although summer is better. June, perhaps?'

'It can be very cold in June,' she murmured. 'We'd better leave it until July.'

'Or August, even. Except everyone will be away. Maybe September would be a possibility…' But she was asleep.

He dropped a kiss on the top of hair silvered by the lights of passing cars. 'September,' he repeated softly. 'September is certainly a possibility. The question is, which September?'

'Hmmm?'

'Nothing, sweetheart. Go to sleep.'

CHAPTER SEVEN

'JULIE, where are the morning papers?' Fergus glanced irritably at the intercom. 'Julie?'

'I'll bring them right in, Fergus.'

He looked up as she opened the door. 'What is the matter with everyone this morning?' he demanded. 'I've been getting odd looks and sudden silences ever since I arrived.'

By way of answer, Julie, her face blandly expressionless, placed a pile of newspapers on the desk in front of them. 'What's this? The press release about the takeover isn't due to go out until—'

'It's not about the takeover. In fact, it's not about the company at all. I've marked all the stories I've seen. Of course, there may be more; I've sent out for the tabloids—'

'Tabloids?' He stared at her. 'What on earth are you talking about?'

Julie's expression remained deadpan as she picked up a financial broadsheet. '"Another Kavanagh Merger",' she read aloud.

'But I thought you said—'

'"This weekend Fergus Kavanagh made one of his trademark takeover bids. With all the panache we have come to expect from the Chairman of Kavanagh Industries, he stunned family and friends by announcing his imminent marriage to Veronica Grant, Marketing Director of the fast growing Jefferson

Sports group of companies. The couple, who both live in Melchester, are said to be planning to wed in November.'''

'What?'

'Don't you just love that ''both live in Melchester'' line? It suggests you're living together without coming right out and saying so.'

'Living together!' She offered him the newspaper to read for himself and in the meantime picked up another, folded back at the 'Diary' column that had been marked for his attention.

'''Kavanagh Takeover Bid'',' she began, then glancing at Fergus over her spectacles, said, 'The headlines all take the same boringly predictable line.'

'You surprise me.'

Julie's eyebrows shot skyward. '*You're* surprised. When I suggested it was time you had some fun, I didn't anticipate you taking me quite so seriously.'

'Julie—' he warned.

She flicked the paper and then began to read. '''The Carteret wedding celebrations were considerably enlivened this weekend by the surprise announcement that Veronica Grant, once reported to be contemplating marriage with George Glendale, the Seventh Earl of—'''

'That's enough, Julie. You can stop right there.' He had no wish to hear any more about George Glendale, his title, or his damned moat.

'''Interesting'', I think you said.' Julie dropped the newspaper on the pile with the others. 'You did not exaggerate. And somewhat sudden.'

'Sudden?'

'Considering you knew so little about the lady on

Friday morning that you were asking for press cuttings. She must have made quite an impression.'

'Yes,' he agreed. 'She did.'

'May I offer you my sincerest congratulations?'

'I'll settle for a cup of coffee,' he replied, noncommittally. The telephone on the desk beside him began to ring. 'And you can answer that. I'm not here.'

She picked up the receiver. 'Mr Kavanagh's office.' She listened. 'I'm terribly sorry, Miss Grant, but I'm afraid that Mr Kavanagh isn't in his office at the—'

Fergus stood up and took the telephone from his grinning PA. 'Coffee, Julie,' he said. Then, 'Please.' He waited until she had closed the door behind her. 'Veronica?'

'Hello, Fergus. I thought you were unavailable?' Her voice teased him, and suddenly things weren't quite so black.

'I've just seen the newspapers.'

'Only just? You didn't read the *FT* over your kippers this morning?'

'No, I decided to drive up to town.'

'Ah.' The word conveyed a world of understanding that the train, Peter and the daily ritual of kippers had not been quite to his taste this morning.

'Julie took great pleasure in marking the stories for my attention, though.'

'Julie?'

'My PA.'

'Yes, well, my Lucy had fun that way too. I was rather hoping she might miss them, but the editor of one of the society gossip magazines telephoned while

I was in an early meeting and left a message asking if they can do a feature on the wedding.'

'Oh, my God—'

'She was rather quick off the mark; they usually wait until there's a formal announcement. Still, now I've seen the papers I can understand her hurry. I have to tell you, Fergus, that my stock with the female staff here is at an all-time high.'

'I can imagine. What did you say?'

'To the society editor? Simply that I was delighted they had thought my wedding important enough to be featured in their delightful magazine, but that I would have to talk it over with you.'

'A simple "no" would not have sufficed?'

'Of course not. They would have assumed I was angling for a higher fee.'

'A higher fee? These people *pay*?'

'Oh, dear, should I have said yes?' she asked. Her laughter was warm and gentle, and quite suddenly he didn't care about the newspapers. Unfortunately, they were impossible to ignore.

'I don't understand how all the papers have the story. One I could understand—I've no doubt that there was someone at the wedding who has a contact—but even the financial papers had a paragraph.'

'I know. Whoever filed the story wanted to be sure that everyone heard the news,' she agreed. 'Now, who is the one person who leaps to mind?' When he didn't immediately answer, she laughed again. And again the world seemed a better place. 'There's no need to be tactful, Fergus. My mother has outdone herself. When you feel overcome by the urge to strangle her, just hold on to the thought that, after your sister's wedding, she will have to call them all again and tell them that it was a mistake.'

'You're going to own up, then? I thought we were going to let this thing run for a while.'

'I know, but—' *But.* He didn't like the sound of that *but* '—there are implications—'

'People will expect to see us together?' he offered, cutting off her objections before she could voice them. 'That had occurred to me, too.' *He'd thought of nothing else all weekend.*

'You don't mind?' She sounded surprised. 'I mean, it's one thing kidding interfering relations, but you have a reputation to consider. I have a reputation to consider…'

'You'd rather tell your mother that it was a hoax?'

'I didn't say that.'

'And then expect her to call the diary editors and explain that the announcement of our forthcoming marriage was a mistake.' Quite suddenly, the newspaper coverage didn't seem quite the disaster he had first thought it. 'Isn't that a little unfair? After all, we made no effort to correct her mistake.'

'With Dora standing right beside her? I thought you wanted her convinced. Well, she's convinced. The whole world is convinced. You don't have to worry about a thing now.'

'I'm very glad you think so,' he said drily.

'It was your contingency plan,' she pointed out. 'You were the one who raised your glass…' It must have occurred to her that she could have objected at that point, and that she hadn't, because all at once she changed tack. 'And once the date was set, my mother was too busy ordering up a crate of champagne—

which you paid for—and telling all and sundry the good news.'

'And Dora had already rushed off to find a telephone so that she could tell Poppy.'

'Have you spoken to Dora or Poppy since Friday?'

'No. Poppy and Richard went home on Friday afternoon, and Dora and John were up in town for the weekend. Neither of them rang.'

'They didn't want to disturb you.' She paused. 'Us. You do realise they will have assumed—everyone will have assumed—that we spent the weekend together.'

'That had occurred to me, but—'

'Oh, Fergus. I'm sorry. I thought this was all going to be so simple.'

'We're in this together, Veronica.' And, for his part, he didn't consider a general assumption that Veronica had stayed at Marlowe Court for the weekend any great cause for regret. His only regret was that it was fiction rather than fact. But maybe she didn't feel the same way.

'We'll have to make a clean breast of this, I suppose. We can't let it go on.' She actually sounded quite disappointed at the prospect, he thought, which was hopeful.

'Whatever you say. Shall I call your mother, or will you?' There was a really promising groan from the other end of the line, and he chose that moment to offer her a temporary reprieve. 'Of course, it would be helpful if you could leave it until after Dora's wedding. That's only two weeks away. Less.' She didn't answer. 'That is, if you're still prepared to come to Dora's wedding.' Julie tapped circumspectly on his door and waited. 'Will you hold on for just a moment, Veronica? Come in, Julie, for goodness' sake.' He waited while she practically tiptoed across his office and put a tray down beside him. 'Thank you. And Julie?'

'Yes, Fergus?'

On the point of saying that he would explain everything later, he changed his mind, shook his head. 'Nothing. I'll buzz you in a few minutes.'

'Fergus?' Veronica's voice was like silk in his ear. 'Are you there?'

'Someone came into the office,' he said. 'So, what about Dora's wedding?'

'Of course I'll come. I promised. And Fergus?'

His grip tightened on the phone. 'Yes?'

There was a moment of hesitation. 'I was just going to say that you're right. After all, what difference will a week or two make? The damage is done, and if we rush to deny it now, people might begin to think there's something really odd going on.'

He had been so sure that the newspapers would have put her off. Ruined everything. Which just went to prove the old saying that there was no such thing as bad publicity. 'If you're quite sure?'

'Quite sure. It's the least I can do after you went to such lengths to be convincing on my behalf. And you were very convincing.'

'Too convincing?'

She didn't comment on that. 'May called me yesterday to tell me how glad she was that I'd made the right decision.'

'Did she?'

'Actually, that was rather an odd thing to say, don't you think?'

'May is a decidedly odd lady.' But he wondered if perhaps they were wrong about Annette calling the papers. May had been the one doing all the pushing. Maybe she'd thought they might need an extra shove…

'You made quite a hit with her,' Veronica said.

'That would have been the large Scotch and the winner at Ascot.'

'That'll do it every time with May.' There was a pause. 'Well, I'll see you in two weeks' time, Fergus. At Dora's wedding. Perhaps you'd let me know the time and place.'

'An invitation is in the post.' He'd dealt with it himself.

'Right. Well, I'll say goodbye, then.'

'Yes. No. No, wait—' She waited. He'd worked all this out over the weekend, but the newspapers had driven everything out of his head; her voice had driven everything out of his head. 'I'm going to a business dinner in Melchester on Wednesday,' he said. 'Do you think it might look odd if you aren't with me?'

'It might. But if it's the Melchester Business Group Dinner, I'll be there, Fergus.'

'On your own?'

'Not exactly. Jefferson's have a table. But if you're going to be on your own why don't you join us?'

This, then, was equality? An invitation to a business dinner from a lady. It was certainly different. 'Thank you,' he said. 'I should enjoy that very much.'

'I'll ring the organiser and ask her to reseat you.'

'No. Don't do that,' he said quickly. 'I'll see to it. I'll pick you up at seven.' Then, because he didn't want her to think he was presuming too much, 'That is if you would like me to?'

'It would look odd if we arrived separately.'

His entire world had become a very odd place indeed since Friday morning, but he didn't intend to argue. 'Seven o'clock?' he suggested.

'Seven o'clock will do just fine.'

Veronica replaced the receiver very gently in its cradle, a small smile playing about her lips. The invitation had been unexpected, and yet she should have known. Fergus Kavanagh was a man whose attention to detail was famous. A man who strove, as she did, for perfection in everything. Which was perhaps why neither of them had ever come close to marriage.

Such a man would hardly overlook something as obvious as the need to be seen in public together. Even games had to be played to win.

'My God, Veronica. You look like a cat with a bowl of double cream and the prospect of smoked salmon to follow,' Nick Jefferson said, coming to a halt in the doorway of her office. 'But then, I suppose in a manner of speaking you are.' He grinned as he dropped a file on her desk. 'Can you spare a moment to look at these proposals? When you can tear your mind away from all those really important decisions about catering and bridesmaids—'

'Hello, Nick. How's Cassie?' she asked, cutting off his nonsense.

'Disappointed not to see you on Saturday. She hasn't seen you for weeks.'

'No. I've been rather busy.' At least she had a genuine excuse for not going to supper on Saturday. 'Will you apologise for me? Fergus brought me home and—'

'I was kidding,' he said gently. 'I'm sure you had a lot more interesting things to do this weekend than play guinea pig for one of Cassie's recipes.' Then he frowned. 'Actually, it's just as well you didn't come.'

'She's all right?'

'Blooming. Full of energy. It's just that she's stopped cooking and taken it into her head that the entire house needs cleaning from top to bottom,' he said.

'You'd better keep an eye on her, Nick, it sounds as if she's nesting,' Veronica said a little anxiously. 'Has she got her suitcase packed for the midnight dash? You need to be ready—'

'Hey, don't worry. Everything is in hand. I've read the handbook for expectant fathers,' he reassured her. 'Twice. Although why these things always happen in the middle of the night beats me.'

'I suppose it's an atavistic, caveman sort of thing. The primitive instinct is to give birth under cover of darkness.' She paused. 'Or at least with the eyes very tightly closed.' She realised Nick was staring at her. 'What?'

'Is this the new, about-to-be-married Veronica Grant? Earth mother? Wise in the ways of womanhood? I never thought I'd live to see the day that you would abandon the boardroom for domesticity.'

'You won't.' She forced the detachment back into her voice. 'And I'm not. You know me better than that, Nick.'

'I thought I did.' He propped himself on the edge of her desk. 'I can't count the number of times I've heard you arguing with Cassie about whether it's possible for a woman to have both a successful career and a successful marriage. Not that you've converted her. Can it be that she's finally converted you?'

'Cassie works from home, Nick, at her own pace, and she has a lot of help. Even so, she plans to cut back for a while once the baby arrives.' And Veronica came back down to earth with a bump as she realised just how far down the fantasy trail she had travelled in the last three days—a trail for ever barred to her. 'It's always the woman who has to make the sacrifice,' she said, switching into feminist mode.

'Raising a family is every bit as worthwhile as running a company, Veronica.'

'That's easy for you to say, Nick. You're not the one carrying the baby.'

Nick's brows rose a fraction at the sudden sharpness of her tone. 'Does Fergus Kavanagh know how you feel, Veronica?' She didn't answer. 'Big estate, family business. I would have thought he'd want—'

'Sons to carry on the family name?' she snapped. 'We are on the edge of the twenty-first century, for heaven's sake…' She stopped as she saw Nick's concern.

'You'd better make sure you have an understanding, then, that the firstborn will inherit. Boy or girl.'

He'd misunderstood her, she realised with relief. 'Yes.' The word caught in Veronica's suddenly dry throat. She tried swallowing. Then, 'We already have an understanding.' *To remain unwed, despite all the best attempts of their relations. She'd better remember that, because she wasn't any wife a man like Fergus would want.* 'Which reminds me,' she said, glad of an excuse to change the subject, 'Fergus will be joining us on Wednesday evening.'

'Us? At our table? At the MBG dinner?'

'That's right. He was going anyway, so I've invited him to join us. There's nothing wrong, is there?'

'Not a thing,' Nick said. 'Although I imagine His Worship the Mayor will be a bit peeved that we've hijacked his guest of honour.'

'Fergus is the guest speaker?'

'You didn't know?'

She was still staring at him when the telephone rang. 'Veronica Grant,' she snapped into the receiver.

'Veronica?'

His voice, so close, so unexpected, made her go suddenly and ridiculously weak. 'Fergus?'

'Is this a bad moment? I can call back—'

'No.' Was her voice shaking? Everything else seemed to be. She took a deep breath, carefully avoiding Nick's eyes. 'No, of course not,' she said, with a commendable stab at briskness. 'What is it, Fergus?'

'I just realised, I don't have your ring size.'

'Ring size?' she repeated stupidly.

'You should have an engagement ring, I think. Just to complete the picture. People...' he paused '...and when I say *people*, of course I mean Dora and Poppy, will expect to see it. At the wedding.'

'Will they?' Then, 'Yes, I suppose they will.'

'Your mother too, of course.'

'Of course.' She couldn't think of anything else to say.

'Do you want to come up to town and choose something yourself, or will you trust my judgement?'

'I can't get away today. Why don't you surprise me?' she invited.

'Well, I thought a plain solitaire diamond, but just say if you'd prefer a coloured stone. A sapphire, perhaps?'

Veronica was finding it difficult to think straight, especially with Nick grinning from ear to ear. 'I…er…'

'Would you like a little while to think about it?'

'No. No, a diamond will be lovely. They…it…will go with everything,' she stuttered inanely.

'And the size?' he prompted.

He was asking her how big a stone she wanted? 'Good grief, Fergus, I don't know—'

'I meant the ring size, Veronica.' He sounded amused, cool, utterly in control. That was her role. She was always the one in control. She'd been in control when she'd picked him up over breakfast; she'd been in control this morning when she'd called him, determined to let him know that the publicity wasn't a problem for her. And that she would make sure it wasn't for him. It hadn't been quite like that, though. And now, with Nick watching her, an eyebrow cocked in amusement at her confusion, she could feel the hot colour surging to her cheeks. She was blushing. *Blushing!* It was impossible; she didn't blush… At least, she hadn't blushed until she'd met Fergus Kavanagh.

'Oh, yes. Sorry. I seem to be…' Wittering. 'I don't know it, Fergus. I'll call you back later,' she said, and hung up quickly. 'Well?' she demanded, as Nick continued to grin in open amusement. 'What's so funny?'

'You, in a dither. I just can't wait to meet the man who can reduce the ice queen to mush.'

'He hasn't. He doesn't...'

'If you were standing on this side of the desk, you wouldn't be saying that.' Then he shook his head, laughing. 'You'll be in that maternity ward faster than a rabbit.'

His words, meant to tease, cut her to the quick. 'You think that's funny?'

'A baby within a year. A crate of champagne on your first anniversary if I'm wrong.'

'Order it now,' she advised.

The ring was beautiful.

He'd called in on his way back from town to give it to her. She'd only just got in from work when the doorbell rang, and she'd assumed that it was a neighbour calling to pick up a box of oddments she'd promised for the church bring-and-buy sale. But it had been Fergus. Distinguished, handsome, in a long dark overcoat, his hair and shoulders sparkling with fine rain, the early promise of summer having disappeared quite as quickly as it had arrived.

'You're going out,' he said, seeing her jacket.

'No. No, I've just got home.' And she stood back. 'Come in, Fergus.' He'd dropped her at her door on Friday night. Walked her right up to it, kissed her cheek and seen her inside. But he hadn't stepped over the threshold. Now he did, and never before had the hall of her cottage seemed quite so small. 'Would you like a coffee? A drink, perhaps?' she offered.

'I'm driving, but a coffee would be most welcome.' He followed her through to the kitchen, where she discarded her jacket on a stool and filled the kettle.

It was odd, but she felt embarrassed. No, not embarrassed; that was the wrong word. Awkward. A little breathless and tongue-tied. Like a teenager with a boy she is desperate to date, but doesn't know how because she hasn't got the vocabulary to start up a conversation, bridge the yawning gulf between them. Nearly thirty years old, with a successful career to which communication was the key, and she couldn't think of a thing to say.

She set out the cups on a tray. Poured milk into a jug. 'Do you take sugar?' she asked. *Oh, brilliant.*

'No.'

'Actually, that's just as well, because I don't think I have—'

'I've brought the ring,' he said, cutting short the stilted conversation. Now that was communication.

Her head came up. 'So soon? I mean…' She wasn't entirely sure what she meant.

'I thought you might like to wear it on Wednesday, and I wanted to be sure it was a good fit.'

'Oh, heavens, yes. I wouldn't want to risk losing it.'

As she was speaking he took a small leather-covered box from his pocket, opened it, took out the ring and the words dried in her mouth.

'It's very simple, but I thought you would prefer that.'

He held the circle of gold between his fingers, the diamond flashing back the light from the spotlights over the island unit, and waited for her to hold out her hand so that he could slide it on to her finger. But her fingers were shaking so much that she had them balled up into a fist.

Deep breath. Nick had called her the ice queen. She could do with a little of that ice right now.

'This is silly,' she admitted finally, 'but my hand is shaking. I've never done this before.'

'Not even with the earl?'

'We never got that far. It was a family heirloom and he was a cautious man...'

Dark eyes seemed to flash like the diamond as he looked down into her face. 'Would you believe me if I told you that mine is shaking, too?' He extended his left hand so that she could see the faintest of tremors for herself, then he reached out and grasped hers, held it for a moment so that they steadied one another as they stared at the ring. 'It seems we're both first-timers at this.'

'I suppose, if you get it right, once is all it takes.'

She looked up, and for a moment their gazes locked and held. Then he slipped the ring on to her finger and bent to brush her lips with his own. The briefest of touches, a formality, over before she had quite registered it.

'It's quite lovely,' she said, on a little catch of breath. And it was. A perfect solitaire. Exactly what she would have chosen if this had been for real. And she felt a tiny clench of regret that it wasn't. Which was ridiculous. This was just a game, a little conspiracy, and she raised her head and looked him right in the face. 'I'll look after it. Give it back.'

'Give it back?' He shrugged, as if he hadn't thought

about that. 'Why don't you throw it back,' he suggested, 'very publicly?'

'Is that how we're going to play it?'

'Why not? We could go to some fashionable London restaurant, the kind of place where you can guarantee anything that happens will be in the newspapers before breakfast time.' He offered a smile. 'I really couldn't put your mother through the nightmare of having to call everyone and explain.'

'That's kinder than she deserves.'

'It's also more likely to be reported,' he pointed out.

'Yes, I suppose it is.' She gave a little sigh. 'Then I'm glad I chose a diamond. It will make a far more satisfactory flash.' She turned the ring again, and it did indeed flash most spectacularly. 'But I'll hate to part with it.'

'There's no particular rush, Veronica.'

'Dora's wedding is less than two weeks away. After that—'

'After that there'll be other weddings. Other family parties. We might as well make the most of it.'

'We mustn't let things go too far. My mother will be organising invitations, getting quotes from caterers—'

'I'll call a halt the moment you say the word, Veronica. I'll book a table at one of those restaurants staked out by the paparazzi and we'll stage a break-up that will make the all the papers—'

'That sounds perfectly dreadful.'

'Well, there's no rush.'

'No, I suppose not.'

CHAPTER EIGHT

VERONICA, who had been turning the ring on her finger, glanced up at him, caught the smile on his face. 'If I didn't know better, Fergus, I would think you're actually enjoying this,' she said rather crossly.

'Would you?' He eased himself out of his coat and hooked it behind the kitchen door before crossing to the kettle, which had just come to the boil and switched itself off. He poured the water on the coffee, perfectly at ease in her kitchen. 'There's no reason why we shouldn't enjoy ourselves, is there?'

'Well, no, but—'

'Good, because I've reserved a box for the new play that's opening at the theatre this Friday.'

'You've done what?'

'If you're free, that is?'

'I'd better not have a date with anyone else, had I?' she said, torn between irritation at his high-handedness and the knowledge that an evening in his company was something she would enjoy. 'Come to think of it, neither had you,' she said. And there were no mixed feelings about that. In fact, the thought gave her a whole lot of pleasure.

'I'm glad you see it that way. Perhaps we could take in a concert too.'

She discovered she was finding it hard not to smile. 'As a sponsor of the local orchestra, it would seem to be your duty.'

'On Saturday, then. After the Cup Final.'

'My social life is looking up.' And she quite suddenly laughed. He always made her want to laugh. 'Why don't we make a weekend of it, spend Sunday afternoon strolling around the museum? I haven't actually seen your mother's potsherds. I ought to, don't you think?'

'Everyone should see them once,' he agreed solemnly, pushing down the strainer on the cafetière and pouring the coffee into two cups.

'Like Venice?'

'As in "see Venice and die"? Don't you think we should save Venice for our honeymoon?'

'My parents went to Venice for their honeymoon.'

'Annette told me. In fact, she thoroughly recommended it. Where would you like to stay? The Danielli?'

This was a game, Veronica reminded herself as she considered his choice of hotel. Just a game. 'Too many marble cherubs,' she objected. 'Besides, I like to ride when I'm on holiday. Venice is a mite short of bridle paths.'

'That's true. What about Tuscany?'

'In November? Don't they get thunderstorms there?'

He grinned at her. 'Are you going to be terribly difficult to please?'

'Terribly,' she assured him. 'We'll probably fight about it.'

'In that case I'll give the matter some thought before making any further suggestions,' he promised, sliding on to a stool. 'But if you like to ride, why don't we make a day of it on Sunday? Come back to

Marlowe Court for supper after the concert and we can ride first thing, swim if it's warm enough, have lunch...and, speaking of food,' he continued, without waiting for her to accept or decline his invitation, 'what had you planned for dinner this evening?'

'I'm sorry?' The pace of the conversation was going a little quickly for her. *Stay at Marlowe Court on Saturday night? Just what exactly did he have in mind?*

'*Had* you planned anything? Or are you one of those working women who doesn't bother much about food?'

She stared at him. 'Are you checking out my qualifications as a wife, by any chance?' she asked sharply.

'Why would I do that?' he enquired easily, as if he hadn't noticed her sudden loss of cool. 'I have a housekeeper who is quite capable of dealing with any domestic chore you care to name. I was simply going to offer to scramble some eggs for us both. With truffles. What do you say?'

Say? 'If you want to know the honest truth, Fergus, I'm lost for words.'

'I'll take that as a yes, then, shall I?' He swallowed a mouthful of coffee and slid off the stool. 'I've got some eggs in the car.'

'I've got plenty of eggs,' she protested.

'Free range eggs from Marlowe Court's home farm?' She lifted her shoulders in a gesture of resignation. 'I thought not. And I picked up the truffles at Fortnum's this afternoon. So why don't you go and put your feet up while I prepare our supper?'

'But...' Veronica was confused. She had preconceived ideas about how men were supposed to behave. This did not even come close.

'Yes?'

'You don't know where anything is,' she said lamely.

Fergus paused in the doorway. 'Is your kitchen so very different from everyone else's?' he enquired.

'Well, no, but—'

'You know, Veronica, I have the strongest feeling that if I even suggested you needed my help to read a balance sheet, you'd snap my head off. Am I right?'

'Probably,' she admitted.

'Equal is as equal does, partner.' Then he grinned. 'You can wash up.'

Veronica didn't put her feet up. Instead, she went upstairs and changed from her business suit into a pair of softly pleated trousers and a toning tunic top. Freshened her lipstick. Brushed out her hair. By the time she came downstairs, her supper was ready. Creamy scrambled eggs, dotted with truffles, were heaped up on two warm plates. A third contained a pile of toast triangles. 'You don't mind eating in the kitchen, do you?' he asked.

'I usually do.' She slipped on to a stool at the breakfast bar on the centre island while Fergus poured her a glass of wine and himself a glass of mineral water.

'This is a real treat. Thank you, Fergus.'

'Any time. Although why you should sound so surprised...'

'Natural scepticism, I suppose. Nick Jefferson once offered to cook for me,' Veronica said, as they ate their way slowly through the toast and the eggs, savouring every mouthful. 'He had a cook hiding in the kitchen all the time.'

Fergus frowned. 'I thought Nick Jefferson was married.'

'Oh, he is,' she said, and turned to smile at him. 'He married the cook.' She bit into the last piece of buttered toast. 'I'm beginning to see the attraction.'

'If that's an attempt to wriggle out of the washing up,' he said, gathering the plates and dumping them into the sink, 'I have to tell you that flattery will do it every time.'

'Oh, no, Fergus—'

But he had unfastened his cufflinks and begun to roll up his sleeves. Then he picked up the drying cloth and offered it to her. 'Diamonds and dishes don't mix.'

'No, I suppose not.' She held out her hand to admire the diamond sparkling on her finger, oddly reluctant to remove it, the smallest of sighs giving her away. But, before she could slip it off, Fergus reached out and caught her hand.

'Leave it.' For a moment it was as if time had stopped. Just a moment when his hand covered hers, when the darkness of his eyes, the silver of hers, seemed to collide and lock, the electricity arcing between them like summer lightning. Even her pulse missed its constant beat.

Then it was over. Her hand was her own once more, he was offering her the drying cloth and it might have been nothing but imagination. 'Leave it, Veronica. I'll wash, you dry.'

They worked in silence. The kind of silence that was heavy with meaning, a silence that a wrong word—or the right one—could fracture, and change lives for ever. She glanced at him as he rinsed off a plate and placed it in the rack. What was it about the man that seemed to stir something deep, almost primitive inside her? Something that she didn't recognise or understand. Something that frightened her just a little. He turned, caught her watching him. 'All done,' he said briskly. Then, 'I'd better go.'

'You won't stay for coffee?' She knew she'd said that too quickly, had sounded too eager. Eager? What on earth was happening to her?

'I've work to do,' he replied. And he'd said that too quickly as well. Whatever was happening, it wasn't just her. Then, 'I spent the afternoon in Bond Street instead of at my desk.'

Confusion and just a little disappointment made her sharp. 'I'm sorry to have been so much bother.'

'Did I say it was a bother?' He reached out as if to touch her, reassure her, but didn't quite bridge the space between them. 'I have a report to write for my stockholders, and you know stockholders; they think they own you.' She smiled politely, but was painfully aware that the smile didn't make it past her mouth.

Fergus unrolled his sleeves and picked up one of his cufflinks. His report, and his stockholders, could have waited until the morning, but he had to get out of this kitchen, and quickly, before he did something stupid, like reaching out and taking her hand, pulling her into his arms in a prelude to making slow, sweet love. Not because he thought she would object. On the contrary, the air was rich, heavy with tension, mute longing. They were two adults in a situation tailor-made for an affair, and her invitation to stay had included more than coffee, whether she had known it at the moment of utterance or not.

All he had to do was reach out, touch her silver-blonde hair and she would be in his arms, and he wouldn't be going anywhere for a very long time.

The temptation was like a fire; it had come from a spark, the idea to call and surprise her this evening with a ring, with supper. Now it was an inferno, burning him from the inside out.

He was resisting for only one reason. Making love with her, delightful though it might be, was not enough. It would never be enough. He'd set out from his home on Friday morning with nothing more on his mind than a determination to avoid matrimony. By Friday night he hadn't been able to think of anything else. He wanted her there beside him when he woke up every morning for the rest of his life. And for that he would have to wait until she wanted it too.

He glanced down at his cuff. Fastening his cufflinks was something he did on automatic every morning of his life, he'd never had to think about it, but suddenly his fingers were refusing to co-operate.

The knowledge that Veronica was watching his fumbling efforts was not helping. 'Are you ready to give up, Fergus?' she asked after a moment.

The cufflink shot from his fingers and flew across the kitchen floor. She picked it up, offered it to him, but his hands were shaking too much to take the wretched thing from her. He was pretty sure she knew that too.

'Give up?' he repeated, stalling for time.

'Give up and admit that your sisters are right.' She folded his cuff back and bent to slip the link through the buttonholes. Her hair slid across his arm and her scent seemed to envelop him. More than just the gardenias in her perfume, this was much more, something that *was* Veronica: the essence of her skin, her hair, her entire body, calling to something deep, something untouched within him. It invaded him with its drugging sweetness and he was ready to admit anything…

She glanced up, her silvered eyes dark and lustrous, and held out her hand for the other one. It was as steady as a rock and he resented that. He wanted her trembling, incoherent, as he was at that moment, with desire. He wanted to take her hand, cradle it in his so that she would know; he wanted to kiss her palm, the pale skin at her wrist, the delicate skin of her inner arm as he drew her into the warmth of his body. Once there, she would feel his need of her. Once there, he would hold her and never let her go.

Instead, he dropped the other link into her palm. 'What on earth are you talking about?' he asked.

For a moment her hand closed on the plain gold link. Then she essayed the smallest of shrugs. 'I thought we had agreed, Fergus, that when a man can't handle his own cufflinks, he needs a wife to take care of him.'

He didn't answer. His sisters knew nothing.

After a moment she folded back the other cuff and fastened it for him. As she leaned across him her hair brushed his cheek, sensuous as silk; the temptation to touch it, lift it and let it fall through his fingers, to stroke the sensitive skin at the nape of her neck, was an exquisite torture. His body stirred, needing her so desperately that he wanted to shout it loud, roar like some savage before he burst, certain that if he didn't take her into his arms that very moment he would go mad.

'Veronica...' But her name was little more than a breath as he whispered it. For a moment she was quite still, as if she was not certain that she had heard, then she looked up and his senses reeled with a raw need to make love with her. To tell her how he felt, that this was it, a once and for ever love—

But somewhere, deep inside him, a klaxon was clamouring a warning that it was too soon. That, even if it was possible that she had fallen in love with him as he had with her she wouldn't believe it. Worse. She wouldn't want to believe it. Her bed might be his tonight for the asking, but he wanted her heart, her soul, her very being...and he wanted them for ever.

He shook his head. 'Nothing,' he said. The word mocked him. 'Just, thank you.' He picked up his jacket and put it on, but he left it unbuttoned. Buttons were beyond him. He took his coat from behind the door. 'I'll see you on Wednesday,' he said.

'At seven,' she agreed, back in control, cool as ever.

And as he sat behind the wheel of his car, glad of the cold night air to chill his heated body, he swore to himself that he would match that coolness; swore that he would not phone her, would not find some other excuse to drop by, that she wouldn't hear from him again a moment before seven o'clock on Wednesday.

Veronica leaned against the door and let out a long, slow breath. That had been close. Asking him to stay for coffee had been a mistake. Fastening his cufflinks had been a mistake.

For a moment it had been a coin-toss whether or not she grabbed him by the shirt-front, backed him up against the fridge and kissed him senseless.

If he had touched her, they would never have made the bedroom.

Which explained a lot about the cufflink-fastening game.

She looked down at the ring glinting on her finger. That was the problem. 'This *is* a game,' she said out loud, because she clearly needed reminding. 'It's just a game of pretend.' So why was desire sapping the strength from her legs? Why was every cell in her body throbbing with unquenched need?

And why didn't she sound more convincing?

'Good morning, Julie.'

Julie pressed a button on her intercom. 'Sally, coffee, please, and hold all calls for the next half an hour.' She followed him into his office. 'This is urgent, Fergus. I had Frankfurt calling all yesterday afternoon. Where on earth did you go?'

'Shopping.'

'Shopping?'

'Diamonds, truffles…you know…the basic necessities of life…'

She raised her eyes to the ceiling. 'You'll have to call them right now, before your first meeting.'

'Of course, Julie. Whatever you say.' He pressed his own intercom. 'Sally, before you get the coffee, will you please order a spray of gardenias to be delivered to Miss Veronica Grant at her office? Jefferson

Sports in Melchester. Straight away.' Then he smiled at Julie. 'Now, what were you saying about Frankfurt?' The buzzer interrupted him.

'What do you want on the card, Fergus?' Sally asked.

'No card.'

'No card?'

That way he would be keeping his promise to himself. 'If she doesn't know who they're from, Sally, there's no message on earth will make any difference.' He glanced at Julie. 'Am I right?' She just shook her head in disbelief. 'Julie apparently disagrees. She has no romance in her soul,' he said, and switched off.

'Fergus—'

'I'm disappointed in you, Julie.'

Julie gave up trying to pin him down to business and instead settled herself on the chair in front of his desk. 'Have you set the date for the wedding?' she asked.

'November seems the favourite. Veronica's mother seems to think it will take at least six months to organise.'

She smiled. 'Can you wait that long?'

'I will if I have to.' He regarded Julie across his desk. 'I'll wait six years if I have to.'

'But surely—?'

'It's a bit complicated, Julie.'

'Is it?' When he didn't continue, she placed a folder in front of him. 'Will this help?'

'What is it?'

'You asked for information on Miss Grant. This is everything I could find.'

He stared at the folder, for a moment laid his hand on the buff manila as if he might absorb through his fingers the essence of the woman, the key that would wind the clock, set her ticking... He recognised a desperation to know everything there was to know about her, everything she had ever done, every place she had ever been, and for a moment his thumb brushed the edge of the folder, flicking at it. Then he picked it up and handed it back. 'Thank you, Julie, but I would be grateful if you would shred this.'

'Shred it? Now?'

He glanced at her, suddenly irritable, impatient. 'No, not now, Julie. Now we have to sort out Frankfurt.'

On Tuesday, Veronica broke with the disciplined habits of a lifetime and bought a new dress for the MBG Dinner.

For the past ten years she had bought her clothes twice a year, building a wardrobe of classics to carry her through any occasion. Simple, well-made clothes that matched and mixed. Clothes that never dated and could be worn again and again.

She had been planning to wear something simple rather than glamorous to the dinner, a black designer two-piece she'd had for ever. Elegant, classic, the straight, ankle-length skirt, and plain, long-sleeved tunic top were perfect for a businesswoman who wanted to be taken seriously. Melchester might be a city, but it had a small-town atmosphere. The men were conservative with a very small c, and their wives were suspicious with a capital S, so under normal circumstances she would have been very careful to dress down for the occasion, wear her hair in a plain chignon, add a little discreet jewellery.

But suddenly things were different, and, walking through the atrium on her way to work, Veronica saw a dress in a boutique window, a dress the colour and texture of an oriental poppy, silky, slightly crumpled, a whisper of a dress that she knew would cling to her figure and shout "look at me". On a woman who had just become engaged to be married that would offend no one. It might even serve to remind the wives that their husbands were now quite safe in her company.

And with any luck Fergus would hear the shout, and he would look at her too.

Marriage might not be on the agenda for either of them, but they were both unattached and over twenty-one. And he was the one who had suggested that they might have fun.

She glanced at herself in the mirrored wall of the lift, eased a wayward strand of hair back into place. She might even wear her hair loose, she thought, and since the only jewellery she would wear would be the diamond on her left hand, all she would get from the Melchester businessmen's wives would be indulgent glances.

That would be a first.

But in the heartbeat it took for the lift to reach the top of the Jefferson tower she had second thoughts. Indulgent glances? When had she ever wanted indulgent glances, for heaven's sake? All she had ever asked was to be taken seriously, treated as an equal. If that meant dressing down, so be it. She glanced down at the smart black and gold bag she was carrying. The dress was a mistake. She'd take it back at lunchtime.

Then, while she was congratulating herself on having kept her head, the gardenias arrived. Six perfect white blooms set against dark glossy green foliage, hand-tied with a white satin ribbon. Was it any wonder that she forgot all about taking back the dress?

Nick paused as he passed her door, attracted by the scent. 'Flowers delivered to the office?' he said as she placed them on her desk. 'Fergus is a man after my own heart.'

'They may be from Fergus,' she said, smiling a little as she adjusted the blooms. 'Or, then again, maybe not.'

'And I'm Charley's Aunt,' Nick said, laughing.

'There wasn't a card,' she pointed out.

'Why would you need a card?' He came in, touched the edge of one perfect petal with the tip of his finger. 'Ah, happy days. I remember them well,' he said. 'Although I have to admit I never thought much beyond roses. The man has style.'

'He can cook too,' Veronica said, unable to resist teasing him just a little.

'Is that right?' He was momentarily startled, then the grin was back, broader than ever. 'Why am I surprised? I always knew that would do it.'

'Then it's just as well you can't cook.'

'Cassie keeps trying to teach me,' he replied. 'We just never seem to get very far.'

Whatever turned you on.

For some people it was cufflinks, for others it was slicing onions... 'Happy days?' she murmured.

'I can't fool you, can I?'

'You never have yet,' she agreed.

He leaned forward and kissed her cheek. 'I wish you as happy as I am, Veronica.'

He didn't wait for an answer, which was just as well. All she could manage was a tear that splashed on the petal he had just touched. A tear? She stared at it, as if unsure what it was.

'Veronica, do you want coffee first, or the mail?'

'What?' She blinked and wrenched herself back from an abyss, a dark, familiar, empty place. It was a place she had vowed never to get close to again, and yet here she was, standing at the edge…

'Veronica? Are you all right?'

She looked up from the flowers. 'Yes. Yes, I'm fine.' Of course she was fine. This was just a game, after all. Truth, Dare, Kiss or Promise. She glanced at the boutique bag lying on the filing cabinet in the corner and couldn't think why she had been going to take it back. 'Bring me the mail first, Lucy. It's time I started work.'

Fergus knocked at her door on the stroke of seven. She was barely ready. Still breathless. With a flush that owed more to excitement than blusher.

She'd changed three times. She'd had her hair done that lunchtime, but she'd since put it up, then brushed it out again like some nervous teenager on a first date instead of a mature, sophisticated woman who could handle any situation life was likely to throw at her. Handle it and toss it right back.

'You look…' Fergus appeared temporarily lost for words '…stunning.' Then, as a gust of wind rattled the roses budding in pots on either side of the door, ruffled his hair, he gathered himself, stepped into her tiny hall and placed a spray of white rosebuds on the table beside her before taking her hands, kissing her cheek.

He was so damned detached, she thought. Taking care to keep his distance. It made her glad she had spent the last five minutes frantically scrambling back into the red dress, brushing her hair loose, painting on the scarlet lipstick, because without it he would never have given himself away and she would never have seen that it was all just an act.

'I would have bet any amount of money that you would be wearing black.'

'Would you?' She picked up the flowers and led the way into the sitting room. 'So obvious, don't you think?' she said, glancing back over her shoulder. She was flirting in a way that would normally have left her blushing. 'Rather as if you're hoping no one will notice that you're a woman in a man's world and that you shouldn't really be there.'

'I'm tempted to say that would be impossible. But you'd think me insufferably glib.'

She lifted the roses to her face. They had that special, very delicate spicy fragrance that the heavy-scented reds could never match. 'Would I?' she asked. 'Why don't you try me?'

Unexpectedly, he laughed. 'I'm not falling for that one.'

'Mmm.' *Better*. 'These are lovely. Thank you. And thank you for the gardenias. They made quite an impression.'

'On you?'

'On everybody. Even Nick. That was the purpose, wasn't it? To impress everyone?'

He shrugged. 'I consider it my duty to keep your stock high with your secretary.'

'Then consider your duty done. Lucy hasn't stopped sighing since they arrived. It's playing havoc with her concentration, and it hasn't done much for her shorthand either.'

'No more gardenias to the office, then?'

Veronica smiled but didn't answer. Instead, she went into the kitchen to run some water for the flowers.

She was flirting with him, he realised, as he had been flirting with her, and Fergus discovered that he didn't much like it. It was too shallow, too sophisticated, too civilised. And he leaned again the architrave, watching her hunt for a vase, fill it, put the roses in it and feather their petals with the tips of her fingers. His feelings for Veronica were not in the least civilised; they were deep, and passionate and raw.

She looked up and saw him watching her. 'Would you like a drink before we go, Fergus?'

'No. Thank you.'

'I don't drink before I speak in public, either,' she said, returning with the roses in a tall glass vase and placing them on a serpentine table where they were reflected in an oval gilt mirror.

'You know about that?'

'Nick mentioned it when I said you would be joining us. You'll find that our table has been combined with the Mayor's this evening, in order to save civic pride.'

'Really? Was that your idea?'

She shrugged. 'I have them occasionally. Sometimes I surprise myself.'

'And not just yourself. You surprised the hell out of me on Friday morning.'

Her smile was suddenly less certain. 'It's just been one of those weeks,' she said, then picked up a long black velvet cloak that lay across the sofa. 'Will you help me with this?'

He took it from her. 'Turn around.' She did, and for a moment they too were framed with the roses in the mirror. Then he lifted the soft cloak over her bare white shoulders and eased her hair over the collar, his fingers briefly brushing the nape of her neck. She shivered, turned quickly to look up at him, her eyes huge and very dark.

'Let's go,' he said abruptly. And, while he still could, he took her arm and headed for the door.

They talked in the car. They talked about the weather. They talked about the speech he was to give that night. They filled the road into the city with nothing, and it was a relief to arrive at the Guildhall at the same time as Nick and Cassie Jefferson.

'Cassie! I didn't expect to see you here.' Veronica gave her a careful hug as they hurried out of the gusting wind into the shelter of the Guildhall. 'What a night. You'd never think it was supposed to be spring.'

'At least it's not raining. Yet. I'll probably leave early, but I couldn't miss an opportunity to meet the man of the moment.' Cassie Jefferson turned to Fergus.

'Fergus, this is Cassie Jefferson. You may have

seen her on television. Cassie Cornwell?' she prompted.

Fergus smiled as he took her hand. 'Of course. I bought my sister one of your books... She's getting married next week, and I'm not sure she's ever learned to do much more than open a tin.'

'Who has time to eat when they're in love?' Cassie replied.

'And this is Nick Jefferson,' Veronica went on quickly, before he could reply. 'Nick, Fergus Kavanagh.'

'Jefferson,' Fergus said, acknowledging his host somewhat stiffly.

'Kavanagh.' The two men sized one another up as they shook hands. There was little to choose between them, matched height for height; only years gave Fergus the edge in authority, stature.

Then, to Veronica's intense relief, Fergus relaxed and smiled. 'Fergus,' he invited.

'Nick.' And Nick Jefferson smiled too. 'Come and meet the rest of the party.'

'What was all that about?' Cassie murmured as they handed their wraps in at the cloakroom. 'They were like a couple of stags preparing to fight over the females.'

'Fergus cooked supper for me the other night and I told him about Nick's little attempt to impress me with his cooking. Perhaps it was a mistake.'

'A mistake?' Cassie turned and looked up at her somewhat thoughtfully. 'I don't think so. I'm sure you knew exactly what you were doing, Veronica.' She stopped briefly, her hand flying protectively to the baby lying beneath her waist.

'Are you all right, Cassie?'

Cassie glanced at her. 'I'm fine,' she said. 'Just a touch of backache.' Then, 'Don't look so worried, Veronica.' And she patted her bump affectionately. 'The infant prodigy isn't due for another two weeks.'

Veronica regarded the glowing Cassie, the size of bump she was carrying before her, and felt distinctly uneasy. 'Are you sure?'

Cassie laughed. 'It's only a twinge, Veronica.'

'What kind of a twinge? I think it's only fair to warn you now that I flunked first aid.'

'That's not a problem. I promise you, I have no intention of giving birth in the Guildhall.'

CHAPTER NINE

FERGUS had been speaking for about fifteen minutes when Cassie got up rather hurriedly.

Veronica glanced up in silent query, but Cassie put her finger to her lips and headed for the ladies'. She watched her uneasily for a moment, then a burst of laughter shook the room. She had no idea what Fergus had said, but any man who was capable of making European Monetary Union something to laugh about deserved her full attention. He got it for about a minute. After that she found herself glancing more and more frequently towards the door.

It could just be that sitting still for so long had aggravated Cassie's backache. Maybe she just needed a little fresh air, or had met someone who recognised her from television and had kept her talking. She tried to concentrate on what Fergus was saying. Then Nick, too, glanced anxiously towards the door, caught her eye, and, without waiting for him to ask, she went to see what had happened to Cassie.

She found her in the ladies' cloakroom, lying with her feet up on an elegant gilded *chaise longue*. Her soaked dress was lying discarded in a heap on the floor and she had been modestly draped in towels.

'Cassie! What's happened—?'

'I just made it before the waters broke.' She managed a smile. 'Don't worry—' *Don't worry!* 'The cloakroom attendant has been brilliant. She's gone to call an ambulance.' *Well, that was all right, then.*

'What about Nick?'

Cassie drew in a sharp breath. 'I thought the ambulance was more important,' she said, what seemed to Veronica like hours later. 'But if you could let him know…' Another pain caught her. *Already? Weren't these things supposed to be minutes apart? A lot of minutes apart?* She glanced at her watch, vaguely aware that she should be timing them although she wasn't entirely sure why.

'Just how long have you been having backache and twinges?' she asked as Cassie reached out and grabbed her hand as the wave of the contraction rose, peaked, receded. 'Stupid question,' she said, to no one in particular. 'Will you be all right here on your own while I get Nick?'

'Go,' Cassie insisted, but still Veronica hesitated, unwilling to leave her on her own.

Then the cloakroom attendant returned. 'Is the ambulance coming?' Veronica asked.

'Just as soon as they can, but—'

Veronica wasn't interested in buts. 'Stay with her. I'm going to get her husband.' And she hitched up the glamorous red dress and ran all the way back to the banqueting hall.

Fergus had finished speaking and his audience was applauding enthusiastically when Veronica burst in through the doors. She had been hurrying, he could see, her face was flushed and almost desperate with urgency, and as she began to weave her way through the tables the applause wavered and died down. 'Nick, Cassie needs you. Now.'

He half rose. 'What is it? Oh, God… Where is she?'

'In the ladies' cloakroom. Someone's called for an ambulance, but I don't think there's much time.'

Nick's response was brief and logical. 'It'll be quicker to take her to the hospital—'

'I'll drive,' Veronica said, relieved for once in her life that someone else was taking control. 'She'll need you.'

'She'll need both of you,' Fergus said, and turned to the suddenly silent banqueting room. 'Is there a doctor here?' No one made a move. It was worth a try, but you didn't get too many doctors at business dinners. 'Get her ready to move. I'll bring the car up to the door,' he said to Veronica.

The weather had got worse, much worse, during the course of the banquet. Leaves, twigs torn from the trees, bowled across the tarmac, caught and stuck wetly against his legs as Fergus turned up his collar and, head down, ran into the teeth of a wind driving the rain across the car park in waves. He hit a puddle, and one of his shoes filled with water, but he scarcely noticed as he backed the car beneath the grand porticoed carriage entrance of the Guildhall. He opened the car's rear door, then hurried inside the building.

'Any sign of the ambulance?' he asked the anxiously hovering porter.

'I just rang again, sir, but a high-sided lorry's blown over on the by-pass and there's been a pile-up—'

He didn't wait to hear more. The attendant opened the door a crack to his knock. 'The car's at the door.

Are you ready to go?' he asked as she widened it a fraction to let him in.

Nick, white-faced, looked up. 'No ambulance?' He shook his head. 'Sweetheart, I'm going to carry you out to the car. There's nothing to worry about. We'll be at the hospital in no time.'

He picked her up, and Veronica wrapped the velvet cloak around her. 'Better take these.' The attendant pushed a pile of more towels into Veronica's arms. 'Good luck,' she called as Fergus held the door and Nick shouldered his way through.

People had begun to gather in the entrance, but the buzz of conversation died away and they fell back to let the party through.

Nick laid Cassie on the back seat and then sat at her head, holding her hand, gentling her as Veronica joined them and shut the door behind her.

Fergus glanced back at them. 'Ready?'

Nick nodded once.

'Gently, Fergus,' Veronica warned unnecessarily. A tray of loose eggs wouldn't have been driven more delicately.

But Cassie had other ideas. 'Forget gently,' she urged. 'Just get there as fast as you can—' Her words ran into a long yell, and Fergus put his foot down, relying on the car to take care of 'gently'. But not even the big Mercedes could disguise the savagery of the gale force gusts of wind that buffeted them as they passed gaps in buildings, flinging the rain at the windscreen almost faster than the wipers could cope with. And it took all his skill, every bit of concentration, to avoid the debris flying across the road, while behind him he was painfully aware of the rising urgency of Cassie's cries.

'Stop, Fergus! Stop,' Veronica cried.

'Now?' he demanded. 'Here?'

'We're not going to make it.'

He pulled over, switched on the hazard warning lights and used his car phone to call the hospital, tell them what was happening. Then, 'Is there anything I can do?'

For a moment, their eyes met above the seat. 'Have you got a torch?'

He flipped open the glove compartment and handed it to her.

'Take Cassie's head, will you? I need Nick here.'

He scrambled over the seat and took Nick's place, his arm propping Cassie up, giving her something to push against, and he took her hand, squeezing it encouragingly, although whether she was aware of him at all he couldn't have said.

'I can see your baby's head, Cassie. You're nearly there.' Veronica's voice was calm. She must be as scared as Cassie, he thought, but she wasn't showing it. Since that momentary look of anguished desperation in the banqueting hall she had been like a rock. 'You've nothing to worry about.'

'Wait until you're lying here before you say that—' Cassie gasped as another wave hit her. 'Remember this, Fergus, when you're—'

'Push now, Cassie,' Veronica encouraged, and Cassie's fingers dug into his hand as she did as she was told. 'Again, Cassie. That's it, brilliant, oh, well done! The head's through.' Then, 'Nick, take over.' She grabbed the torch from him.

'What?'

'There, look!' And she slid out of the way as first one shoulder and then another was delivered, leaving Nick to catch his newborn child in his hands. He turned the infant over, wiped its face with the fresh towel Veronica handed him.

'Oh, Cassie,' he said, 'she's so beautiful. She's just like you.' There were tears in his eyes, Veronica saw, tears of pure joy and the kind of pride that made a man want to beat his chest and roar. 'Thank you—' His voice cracked with emotion.

Fergus eased Cassie up a little so that she could see, and Nick lay the baby gently on her abdomen so that she could touch her.

There were tears pouring down Cassie's cheeks too, he saw, and he was pretty close to them himself. Only the flashing blue light of the ambulance saved him. 'It's the cavalry,' he said, easing himself back over the seat as Nick took his wife in his arms, getting out of the car to wave them down.

'In a bit of a hurry, were you, ma'am?' one of the paramedics said cheerfully as he dealt with the placenta, cut the cord and put the baby into her mother's arms. 'That was nice and easy.'

'Why do men always think it's easy?' Cassie said. 'If it's so easy, why don't they do it?'

'We're just not bright enough,' he said, easing her, with Nick's help, on to a stretcher. 'All right? Good. Don't worry, we'll have you tucked up in bed with a cup of tea in no time.'

'Veronica! Fergus!' Cassie shouted as she was lifted into the ambulance. 'I want you to be godparents—'

'You've got it,' Fergus called back. Then the door was shut and they were gone, blue lights flashing as they raced away in the direction of the hospital. 'I have to say, Veronica, when you invite a man out on a date you certainly know how to show him a good time…' he said, turning to her. Then he realised that it wasn't just rain pouring down her cheeks. There were tears, too. 'Veronica? What—?'

'Don't say anything.' She stepped back as he reached for her. 'Don't. Please. Just take me home.'

It wasn't a request to be ignored. Something was wrong, desperately wrong, but this wasn't the place to find out what it was. He opened the car door for her while she climbed in. Then he got in beside her, started the engine and drove slowly back to her cottage.

Maybe it just was delayed reaction. Shock. He glanced at her. The rain had plastered her hair to her head and the bones of her face stood out, sharp and tense. It was as if she was determined to keep all expression from it, show no feeling. She was feeling, all right, but it was not the ecstatic, over-the-moon sense of accomplishment she should be feeling right now.

It was pain. A pain so intense, so shocking, that she was hanging on for everything she was worth, terrified that if she once let it out she would never be able to put that cool, collected image back in place and fool the world.

And his own cold pit of despair beckoned as he began to suspect what it was.

He brought the car to a halt outside her cottage.

'Don't get out—' she began, but he was ready for that.

'I really need to wash my hands.' He didn't wait for an invitation, but climbed out, opened her door and took her elbow to help her out. It might not be PC, she might tell him that she didn't need anyone to help her, but right now she would be wrong.

Her body was rigid, as if she was trying to stop that from feeling too, and for a moment she didn't move. Then, like an automaton, she unfolded herself jerkily from the seat, quite deliberately detached herself from him and led the way to the front door.

She unlocked the door, reset the alarm. 'The cloakroom's through there,' she said abruptly.

He wanted to take her, hold her, tell her that he thought she was truly wonderful and that he loved her with every fibre of his being, but it was as if she were surrounded by one of those invisible shields they had in old science fiction programmes on the television.

And then it was too late to do anything as she looked at her hands, still bearing traces of her brush with midwifery, and, with a groan, made a dash for the stairs.

He took off his sodden jacket, pulled his tie loose, washed his hands and splashed cold water on his face. When he emerged, Veronica hadn't reappeared. But he could hear the sound of water running.

He tossed his jacket on the sofa and searched the living room, found a bottle of brandy in a cupboard and poured some into a glass. She had still not reappeared, and after a moment he carried the glass up the stairs.

The door stood open on her bedroom. It was like

her: restrained, elegant, with pale colour-washed walls, fresh garden flowers in a tall straight-sided glass, little groups of fat white candles, the small casement windows with thick cream calico curtains. And, dominating the room, the glowing walnut of an antique French bateau bed, covered with an old hand-pieced English quilt. The bathroom was beyond it, the door partly open, but the light hadn't been switched on, and the only sound above the wind and rain was that of water running.

'Veronica?' Nothing. He tapped at the door, pushing it wider. She was sitting on the floor, propped against the side of an old-fashioned, lion-claw bath; her face was deathly white, her hair damp in the light spilling in through the open door, and tears were still coursing down her cheeks. 'I thought you could do with a brandy,' he said, stepping through the door, turning off the taps. 'And I was right. Here,' he said, taking her shaky hands, clean but wet, wrapping them around the glass and holding them there with his own. 'Drink it,' he insisted, and as if she were a child, not quite sure what to do, he lifted the glass and held it to her lips, tipping it so that she had no choice but obey him.

She swallowed and coughed, and for a moment life flashed back into her eyes, and with it pain. 'What is it?' he demanded, before she could collect herself, retreat behind the glass wall. 'What's wrong?' Then, because it had to be faced, as all life's pain had to be faced sooner or later, 'Is it Nick Jefferson? Are you in love with him?'

What else could have affected her so profoundly?

'No!' She was genuinely startled. Her denial came

back at him fast and true, and relief surged through him. Not that, then. Not that.

She shook her head. 'How could you have thought it?' she demanded. She liked Nick as a colleague and as a friend, but she could never have fallen in love with him. She had thought, safely wrapped up in her work, that she would never fall in love again. But she had been wrong.

I love you.

Veronica longed to say the words, to tell him, to show him. Instead, she lay her forehead against his wet shirt and began to weep in great grieving, silent sobs that shook her entire body. He took the glass from her, put it down on the floor beside her, and he held her, his arms tight about her, his face against her hair.

I love you.

The words were there in her head, but she couldn't say them, mustn't... He mustn't ever know. It wouldn't be fair... But, as a another fierce gust of wind shook the windows, she moaned and clung to him.

For a moment he held her, then he eased her away while he was still capable of coherent thought. 'Come on,' he said. 'Let's get you out of this dress and into bed.'

'It's ruined,' she said, looking down at her dress, at herself. 'What a mess.' *What an understatement. How had she let things ever get to this point?*

'You're wet through.'

'So are you.' She laid her palm against the cold wetness of his shirt. Beneath it was life, warmth, the beating of his heart, and she raised her lashes, clumped together by rain and the tears she had shed, and looked up at him.

He swallowed. 'You'd better get into something warm, Veronica.'

'I have just the thing.' She looked beyond him to the bed, and then back up into his face. 'Don't leave me, Fergus. Stay with me tonight.'

Stay with her. It was an emotional response to the birth of Cassie's baby, the elemental forces of the storm raging beyond the window. He knew it—knew it, but it would have taken a man of stone to resist her heartfelt plea. And he wasn't stone. He wasn't even clay; he was pure putty as he took her face between his hands, looked into her eyes and discarded without hesitation all those resolutions about making her wait. She needed him. He didn't know why, and right at that moment he didn't care. It wasn't a time for the head, but the heart. 'I'm not going anywhere, darling.' Not tonight, not ever. And his mouth came down on hers with a fervent, precipitate, breathless need. He was past pretence, past playing sophisticated games. He loved her, and right now there was only one way to show her how much.

Her response was instant meltdown, her mouth, hot and demanding, provoking an explosive chain reaction, a no-holds-barred volcanic eruption of desire that leapt between them and surged through his veins like hot lava. She grabbed at his shirt-front, scattering studs as she tugged it open. He hooked down the straps of her gown, peeling the sodden cloth from her skin until he encountered the fastening of her bra. He unclipped it and it fell to floor, but now his hand cradled and warmed the sweet mound of her breast while his mouth explored the hollows of her throat and his other hand, low on her back, drew her into him.

She leaned back, boneless in his arms, keening urgently, desperately. 'Fergus—' she begged.

'I know, darling, I know.' And they ripped at their clothes in a frenzy as the storm raged and tore at the cottage. Then there was a crash somewhere beyond the garden and the lights went out. Startled, she cried out, but he took her cry into his mouth, pulled her hard against him so that she felt the throbbing heat of his need, and the cry became a moan, desperate with a longing as fierce as his own. That was when he picked her up and carried her to bed.

For a moment she lay back against the pillows, her damp hair drying in curls about her face, and in the silent flash of lightning that lit the room she looked more like a girl than the sophisticated woman who had waylaid him with her hatbox, teased and flirted with him. Thunder crashed ominously above them. *I love you*, he said, but inside his head. *You'll never know how much because I don't know the words that can make you understand. I'm not even sure there are words…*

Then she reached for him, stroking her palms up across his chest, his shoulders, his neck, until she held his face between her hands. 'Love me,' she whispered. Outside, lightning flashed again, and in the harshness of the light he saw her eyes, no longer silvered and teasing but swirling with storm clouds that matched the intensity of those boiling overhead and swimming with tears. 'Love me and make the world go away.'

* * *

The storm passed. Fergus lit the candles and, propped up on his elbow, watched her sleeping.

She slept like a child, still and quiet, her mouth smiling as if she, and only she, knew some enormous secret. After a while she stirred, stretched, and as her toes encountered his her eyes opened wide. Then, as she came fully awake, the smile faded and was replaced by an expression of such profound sadness that he was moved to say, 'You do realise that you'll have to marry me, now.'

She became deeply still. 'Marry you?'

He'd done entirely the wrong thing. He knew it instantly. 'Now you've seduced me you're just going to have to make an honest man of me. My sisters will insist. Shotguns at the ready if necessary.' He saw the mixture of emotions chase across her face—disappointment, sorrow, and perhaps a touch of relief as she realised that he had been teasing her. Then, from some deep well of strength, she managed to find a smile to match his nonsense.

'How will they know unless you tell them?'

'I tell them everything.'

'Maybe, but it isn't always the truth. You've told them that we're engaged,' she reminded him.

'We are.' He lifted her left hand, held it over his so that she could see the engagement ring sparkling on her finger. 'You've got the ring to prove it.'

'Fergus, you know that was just a misunderstanding.' She was beginning to sound just a little desperate, which gave him the confidence to press on.

'The misunderstanding was other people's.' He kissed her fingers before turning them over, kissing her palm, her wrist. 'I knew exactly what I was doing.'

'Don't!' She sat up, pulling her hand away, the quilt up to her chin. Then, staring straight ahead, 'I'm sorry.'

'Was I that bad?'

'What?' She turned, startled.

'It's been a while, I'll admit, but I always thought it was a bit like riding a bicycle—' He stopped as tears welled up in her eyes. 'Oh, hey, come on.' He sat up beside her and put his arms about her, gently, so that she would know that he wanted nothing more than to comfort her. 'Poppy and Dora aren't so terrible. Really. They won't make you marry me. Even if you got me pregnant…'

It was silly stuff; it was supposed to make her laugh. Instead, the floodgates opened. She must have been bottling up the tears for a long time, because they poured from her in a silent tide that seemed to go on for ever before she was finally shaken by a great racking sob that broke the last shred of her self-possession, reserve, and she clung to him as if afraid she might drown.

He held her, rocking her against his chest while the storm of tears raged within her that he thought would never end. He gentled her, murmured the soft, meaningless words of comfort, stroking her hair, kissing her forehead, feeling her pain, hurting all the more because he could not ease it.

But, like the storm that had passed over them in the night, hers too gradually subsided, dwindled to involuntary little sobs and hiccups. Then she reached for the corner of the sheet and dried her face, gave a little sniff. 'I'm sorry.' He said nothing, merely tucked the quilt around her more tightly, held her close so that she wouldn't have to look at him. 'It wasn't you...anything you did.'

'I know. It was Cassie, the baby...' Something else.

'I can't have babies, Fergus...' She spoke so quietly that for a moment he didn't quite catch what she'd said. Then the words sank into his brain like a firebrand.

She had known that, and had accepted it, and had forged a career for herself and never let the world see how much she was hurting. Then, tonight, fate had thrown a spanner in the works and all that careful poise and control had snapped.

'But your mother...the biological clock...'

'Broken beyond repair.'

He sat back, stared at her. 'My God, your mother doesn't know, does she?'

She shook her head. 'This way she can blame me for not getting married, for not being a proper daughter, a proper woman...' Her words ate at him. This was what she had been feeling, holding in? For how long?

'Instead of blaming herself? Why would she do that?'

'Because she travelled the world with my father and left me at home in boarding school. She loved him, Fergus. I don't want her to feel guilty for wanting to be with him. It probably wouldn't have made any difference anyway...'

'Can you tell me about it?'

The still light from the candles was reflected in her silver eyes as she raised heavy lids to look at him, testing his sincerity. Then she gave a little sigh. 'I told you I was going to marry a man called George Glendale.'

'The guy with the title?'

'We met at university, but I was a first-year, he was just graduating—older, glamorous and moving on. Then we met again in London. I'd just started my own marketing company. He was bright, clever, with a meteoric career in banking ahead of him. We were a golden couple, our lives a shining path ahead of us. Then he was given an overseas posting—New York—and because he couldn't bear to leave me behind he asked me to marry him.'

She looked up at him, as if uncertain whether this was something he wanted to hear. 'Go on.'

'He took me to Scotland to meet his mother, the Countess Glendale.'

'At the castle?'

'At the castle. It should have been daunting, but it wasn't.' She managed a smile. 'It wasn't a very big castle.' Another small sigh escaped her. 'The Countess was charming and we did the whole family thing—you know, the photograph albums, stories of the scrapes George had got into as a boy…the day he had been rushed to hospital with appendicitis.'

Something in her voice warned him that this was where it had stopped being a pleasant weekend. 'Appendicitis?'

'I thought it was funny—you know, cute—because the same thing had happened to me.' Except it hadn't been quite the same. Her parents had been overseas, she had been at boarding school, and when she had gone to Matron, clutching her stomach with pain, the woman had just dosed her up with syrup of figs and told her not to make a fuss. And she hadn't. Instead, she'd collapsed very quietly in class two days later with a ruptured appendix.

'George's mother didn't say anything until we were on our own, but then she insisted that I go to a gynaecologist and have a check-up.'

His face creased in a frown. 'Why? I don't understand.'

'I didn't understand either. At the time, no one had thought to mention that I might have problems when I wanted to have children.' But the countess had known. 'Apparently there was a risk that because of the rupture I might have sustained damage to my Fallopian tubes.' She was saying this very carefully, so that he would understand that it was serious, that she wasn't making a fuss about nothing. 'That would mean my eggs couldn't be fertilised.'

'Would that have mattered? If he loved you?'

'George was—is—an earl. Countess Glendale made it quite clear that without the possibility of an heir, marriage to her son would be impossible.'

It was hard to suppress his anger, but he did it, for her. 'Children are not guaranteed, Veronica. And even when they arrive they have a fifty-fifty chance of being girls.'

'An even chance, Fergus. That's all she wanted for George. Not no chance.'

'And if you hadn't found out before the wedding? How long would she have waited before she ordered a divorce? What century is she living in, for heaven's sake? And didn't sweet George have anything to say on the subject?'

'I didn't mention it to him. I didn't for one moment think there would be any reason for him to ever know. I went back to London after the weekend, told my doctor the whole story and he arranged a special test—an HSG, he called it—to check if I'd have problems. The countess, it seems, knew her stuff.' She shivered.

'You're cold.' He fished beneath the pillows for a nightgown, then put it over her head, threaded her arms through it, but she was still shivering. It wasn't the temperature that was chilling her. He pulled her down beneath the covers and wrapped his arms around her. 'Come on, you might as well tell me everything.'

'There's nothing more to tell. I explained the situation to George and then offered him the chance to walk away.'

'He took it?' The words came out on a hiss of breath. He couldn't believe any man could be so cruel. 'Dear God, weren't you enough for him?'

'Don't be hard on him, Fergus. In his position—'

He put his hand over her mouth. Then, as she stared up at him with wide, startled eyes, he said, 'Don't even mention him in the same breath as me. I love you. I want to marry you. *You*, Veronica. Live with you, share your life and whatever goes with it, good and bad.'

'Marry me?'

'I'm in love with you,' he said. 'It seems the logical thing to do.'

'But your name—'

'You think the world is short of Kavanaghs?'

She shook her head. That wasn't what she meant

and he knew it. 'Marlowe Court? Kavanagh Industries?' she reminded him. 'Who'll take your place?'

'Kavanagh Industries is a public company. It doesn't need a Kavanagh to survive. As for Marlowe Court—I have two sisters. Poppy has a baby son; Dora will have a stepdaughter the moment she marries John. The next generation is taken care of. Have you any more objections?'

'Of course I have. You scarcely know me. We met less than a week ago, for heaven's sake. You can't possibly want to marry me.'

She hadn't said yes, but then she hadn't said no, either.

And she hadn't said, I don't love you.

'It's a Kavanagh thing,' he said. 'I don't pretend to understand it, but it seems to work.' And he smiled down at her. 'Don't worry, you've got six whole months to get used to the idea.' Her smooth, high forehead was disturbed by a frown. 'November,' he reminded her. 'Your mother is already hard at work organising our wedding.'

'But that was—' He raised a finger to his lips. 'But it was—' He placed the finger on hers. 'No. This is quite—' he tried a kiss '—ridiculous,' she mumbled.

'Then why aren't you laughing?' But he didn't wait for an answer. Instead, he kissed her again, and this time he made sure he put a stop to her objections for a long time.

CHAPTER TEN

WHEN Veronica woke it was light and the sun was streaming in through the bedroom window as if last night's storm had never happened. And she was alone. For a moment she thought, hoped, that the whole thing had been a terrible, a wonderful dream.

But the air was sharp with the scent of burned-down candles, and in the bathroom her ruined dress lay in a damp bundle on the floor. And the shirt that Fergus had been wearing had gone. Had he gone too? Then she heard him downstairs and her heart gave a treacherous, telltale leap…a bound of pure joy, and, without stopping to tell herself that she was living in a fool's paradise, she pulled a wrap from behind the door and rushed down to the kitchen, stopping suddenly in the doorway. Shy.

He turned as he heard her. 'Hello, sleepyhead. I was going to bring you breakfast in bed.' He placed a pot of coffee on a tray already laid with fruit and yoghurt and freshly made toast.

His chin was dark with the overnight growth of his beard, his hair was rumpled, his shirt unbuttoned, creased, and showing the scars left in her eagerness to divest him of it the night before. She could have looked at him for ever. 'I should be at work.'

He grinned as he poured coffee, held out a mug. 'Relax, sweetheart, we're going nowhere until the workmen have shifted a tree that's blocking the end of the road.'

She took it, regarding his crumpled shirt, creased trousers. 'Did you go outside looking like that?'

'I needed to use the phone—yours is out, so I used the one in the car—but don't worry, I didn't go further than that. It was your next-door neighbour who told me about the tree.'

'Mrs Rogers?'

'That's right. Nice lady. Wanted to stay and chat.'

'I'll bet.'

He grinned again. 'Anyway, it was the tree that brought the telephone lines down.'

'I was going to phone the hospital. See how Cassie—'

'Done. Mother and baby doing just fine. We'll go and see them later. And I called your office to explain why you'd be late. You are not the only one, apparently.'

'Is there anyone in the entire world who doesn't know you spent last night in my bed?'

He buttered a piece of toast and offered it to her. 'I'm sure there are a few. But I'll call the local radio station and have them make an announcement if you like. Invite the entire city to the wedding.' His eyes were laughing. He was happy, she realised. And for the first time in as long as she could remember she realised that she was happy too.

'Why don't you do just that?' she said as she held his wrist and bent to take a bite out of the toast. Then, without letting go, she headed back towards the stairs.

'And, since neither of us are going anywhere, you can tell them you're going to spend the morning there too.'

Veronica was fine until she reached the hospital. All afternoon at the office she'd been absolutely fine. Everyone had wanted to know about Cassie's baby, what had happened, and that had been fine too. She'd even had a call from a local newspaper reporter, who was writing a feature on the storm and wanted a photograph of the lady who'd delivered a baby in the back of a car because the ambulance hadn't been able to make it in time. She'd gone down to the atrium and bought flowers and fruit for the new mother, and she had even gone into a baby boutique and bought the infant a gift without cracking up.

Then Fergus had picked her up from work and driven her out to the hospital, and she had held the tiny new life that she had helped to bring into the world and that had been just fine as well. Fergus loved her. She loved him. Life was suddenly, unexpectedly, unbelievably wonderful.

'Have you decided on a name yet?' Veronica asked.

'I ought to call her after you.'

'Don't you dare! Better call her Gilda—you very nearly gave birth in the Guildhall, despite your promise.'

'If that's the criterion, she should be called Ringroad,' Fergus said. 'Or what about Mercedes?' They all looked at him for a moment, as if considering the possibility, before shaking their heads.

'She doesn't look like a Mercedes,' Cassie said. 'She looks like a little flower.'

'But what flower?' Nick took his baby daughter

into his arms. That was when Veronica saw the look in his eyes—warm, tender, full of wonder.

The tiny sound that came from her throat was heard by no one but Fergus. 'We'll leave you to rest, Cassie,' he said quickly, taking her arm.

'But you've only just arrived.'

'You don't need us.' He bent quickly to kiss Cassie's cheek. 'I'll see you, Nick.' And he had her outside the door, was holding her before she could think, his arms tight around her as if he would protect her from the world. 'Don't say anything. I love you.' She didn't doubt it any more than she doubted her love for him. But sometimes love meant sacrifice. His or hers? There was, could only ever be, one answer.

At least this time it would be her decision. Not now. Not today. After Dora's wedding, she promised herself. She would tell him then that it had been a mistake. That she couldn't possibly marry him, that it had simply been an over-emotional response to Cassie's baby, to the storm. By then he, too, would have had time to think more clearly, and she didn't think he would argue. 'All right now?'

She nodded. 'I'm fine.' He didn't look convinced. 'Really. Just a bit emotional, that's all.'

'So, what shall we do this evening? We can eat out, if you like.' She shook her head. 'Then the only thing to decide is your place or mine?'

She knew she should say neither. That she had work to catch up on. It would be the wise thing to say. But she would have the rest of her life to congratulate herself on her wisdom, to catch up on work; she had just a little over a week to store up precious memories. She would make the most of them. 'Mine,' she said. 'And this time *I'll* cook for you.'

It was the second wedding in two weeks, and once again all eyes were on her. But this time, as she stood and turned as the organist struck up the Wagner wedding march, it was not the ethereally lovely bride she was watching, it was Fergus as he led his younger sister up the aisle to give her to the man she loved. It was a moment of great joy, and she blinked back a tear but didn't try to hide it; tears, after all, were perfectly acceptable at a wedding. She simply lifted a delicate handkerchief to her face to blot it away, her smile never wavering for a moment.

And afterwards at the reception, when she was asked about the date for her own wedding, well, Fergus seemed always to be at her elbow with a ready answer.

'November, unless I can persuade Veronica to make it earlier.'

And she had her answer too. 'Earlier? I don't know how I'm going to manage it in six months,' she said. 'Dora will tell you how much there is to do, and she wasn't working.'

'But you'll give up your job, surely? You'll be eager to start—'

And that was another cue for Fergus. 'Certainly not. I'm the one who's giving up work. What's the point of marrying a successful career woman if I don't allow her to keep me?'

It provoked laughter, as it was meant to, and Fergus, with a reassuring squeeze of her hand, moved on, introducing her to family and friends. And there were so many people, all of them strangers. At least at Fliss's wedding Fergus had met people he'd already known. He'd had fun. But it had all been a game then, and the game was nearly over.

There was only one move left, a last desperate throw of the dice. She needed a double six, but she knew the odds were stacked against her...

'I think we could leave now and no one would miss us,' Fergus said. They had been dancing, but now he stopped, still holding her close. Dora and John had been waved away on their honeymoon; Poppy and Richard had taken Sophie along with their own infant son back to their cottage. 'This lot will party all night.'

She looked up at him. 'You don't want to party?'

'Only with you.' And he leaned forward, kissed her lightly on the mouth. For this he received a cheer from the youthful element, who had been enjoying his hospitality with more enthusiasm than sense. Fergus turned and offered them an ironic bow. Then, 'Let's get out of here,' he said. 'I'm far too old to make a fool of myself in public.'

'What about in private?' she teased.

'No objections at all.'

Outside, the twilight garden seemed a peaceful place after the marquee, scented with honeysuckle and early roses. They walked for a while in silence, then Fergus said, 'How do you feel about going away for a few days, Veronica?'

It would be heaven. But a kind of hell, too. And she'd promised herself that this week she would book that restaurant, stage that fight, throw back his ring. And if she did it well enough he would never know that it had all been an act. 'I don't think I can just at the moment, Fergus. I'm just so busy—'

But he was prepared for that. 'If it's work you're worried about, I've already cleared it with Nick.'

She came to an abrupt halt. 'You've done what?' she demanded, but didn't give him a chance to repeat what he'd said. 'When did you see Nick?'

'I didn't. He phoned me. Cassie just wanted to be sure that we knew she meant it when she asked us to be godparents. The christening is six weeks on Sunday. That's if they've decided on a name for the baby by then. You'd think after nine months they'd at least have a shortlist...'

'Nicola. They're calling her Nicola Rose...' Then she realised that she'd been sidetracked, and didn't like it. She had wanted an excuse to be angry with him. Well, now she'd got it. 'And don't think you can change the subject. My job is nothing to do with you, Fergus. Nick is on leave, and right now he doesn't know what day of the week it is, let alone what I've got in my diary. I'm up to my eyes with plans for the launch of a new range of fishing tackle—' Oh, heavens, that sounded so *lame*. The fishing tackle would keep for a few days, but there was something else that couldn't, something she wasn't going to tell him about.

'Fishing tackle? Bring some with you. We'll be staying by a great fishing river.'

'You're not listening to me, are you?'

He might be listening, but he wasn't taking any notice. He was too busy kissing the sensitive spot just behind her ear that he had discovered made her giggle. They were supposed to be having a row, for heaven's sake! She concentrated hard, refusing to co-operate, determined to up the stakes. '*You* couldn't just take a few days off in the middle of something important.' A little feminist hackle-raising might help. 'Just because I'm a woman—'

'That certainly helps,' he said, his mouth deepening at the corners as he looked at her in a way that made her insides melt. Then he lifted an eyebrow. 'Did you just stamp your foot, Veronica? It's a waste of time on grass, you know.'

Not only was he refusing to argue with her, he was laughing at her, and she knew she should be furious, but it was so hard… 'I can't go anywhere this week, Fergus. I've got meetings in London…' his mouth teased across her lips '…and Birmingham…' she protested, but his long, sensitive fingers were gentling the nape of her neck. Then, on a betraying little moan, 'Maybe Friday—'

'What about Friday?'

'Maybe I could…manage…Friday.'

'Only maybe?' His thumb was tracing the line of her hair, and she leaned back into his touch and his lips began to trace a line from her mouth, across her chin and down her throat…

'Definitely,' she promised.

'And Monday?' he pressed.

'Yes, yes.' She gasped the words out as her legs began to buckle. He caught her to him. 'And Monday.' She collapsed against him.

'You know, I have the feeling that if I kept that up long enough you would promise me anything.'

She raised her head and looked at him. 'You know,' she murmured huskily, 'I think you could be right.

But it would be a waste of time right now… A long weekend is all I can manage, really.'

One side of his mouth lifted in a smile. 'I believe you. We'll fly. It will save time.'

'Fly? Where are we going?'

He took her arm and began to walk. 'Only as far as Wales. Just across the border, in fact. Have you been there?' She shook her head. 'It's green and peaceful and quite unbelievably beautiful. Rather like you, Veronica.'

'I'm green and peaceful?' she joked, but it was impossible to disguise the tremor in her voice.

He reached out, touched her cheek, gently rubbed the edge of his thumb along her jawline. 'Did I ever tell you that you have a smart mouth, Veronica Grant?'

'No, but I'm susceptible to compliments.' And his kisses. She was terribly susceptible to his kisses and he knew it. He'd just melted away all her objections, all her justifiable irritation, with the heat of his mouth, the touch of his hand. And he'd barely started…

'How susceptible?'

She turned and closed her eyes over the film of tears threatening to overwhelm her. 'Try me,' she invited.

'Miss Grant? The doctor will see you now.'

He waited until she was seated, but he didn't waste time in small talk. He told her, without dressing it up in frills or offering false hope, that the HSG he had performed only confirmed what she had been told years before. Her Fallopian tubes were damaged; it was impossible for her eggs to be fertilised. She could never conceive without the aid of a test tube.

He began to explain the procedures, but she stopped him. She had met women who had been through that, spent years of their lives obsessed with the desperate need to have a child. She'd seen marriages fall apart under the strain of it all.

She understood; she sympathised. If she had married George, she knew she would have done anything so that he could have had his chance of an heir, but this was different. And she loved Fergus too much to put him through that. But somehow she would have to convince him, when she walked out of this relationship, that it had nothing to do with the fact that she couldn't have his child, and the sooner the better.

Except that her life seemed to be heaped up with complications. There was the christening of Nick and Cassie's baby at the end of June. She couldn't do anything until after then; it would hardly do for the godparents to be glaring at one another over the font.

She had six-weeks' grace to think of something convincing, to distance herself, ease herself gradually away. But first she had the weekend, and she was determined that it would be perfect, a memory to treasure for both them.

'She took that well,' the nurse said, picking up the box of tissues she had left on the doctor's desk in anticipation of tears.

'She's a very controlled young woman, and, to be honest, I don't think she expected to hear anything different from what I had to tell her.'

'Did you tell her that occasionally the HSG procedure can result in restored fertility?'

He glanced at his nurse, shook his head. 'It's rare,' he objected.

'Still—'

'It would be unkind to raise her hopes. Did you give her the literature on IVF?'

'She wouldn't take it.'

The pilot was flying the helicopter low over the flat, grassy floodplain of a small river. They'd skirted Abergavenny and Crickhowell, but now they were apparently miles from anywhere, and Veronica, not particularly happy in small planes of any kind, was finding the all-round view particularly unnerving.

'Where on earth are we?' she asked anxiously. 'There isn't a village, or a town, or even a house as far as I can see.' Then she groaned. 'Don't tell me this is a boating holiday? I warn you, Fergus, I get seasick crossing Waterloo Bridge—'

Fergus took her hand, held it between both of his. 'Not a boat,' he promised. 'And not a tent,' he added, anticipating her next question. 'There. That's where we're going.'

Veronica looked about her, but could see no cottage, no house, not even a hotel tucked away in the quiet countryside. All she could see was a... She turned on Fergus. 'You can't have... You wouldn't... Fergus, please—'

'Please, what? Tell you that I haven't bought a castle?' He shrugged carelessly. 'Okay, if it'll make you happy. I haven't bought a castle.' She gave a sigh of relief. 'But I'm thinking about it, which is why we get to stay here for the weekend. Actually, it's not officially listed as a castle; it's just a watch-tower. Not much more than a fortified turret that was extended in the eighteenth century by some gentleman for use as a fishing lodge. Not even a moat, d'you see?'

'No moat?' He couldn't really be thinking of buying this. He couldn't be that crazy, could he? She was afraid she knew the answer to that. Hadn't they both been acting like idiots since the moment they met? 'Since I don't imagine it's got a damp proof course, that's probably just as well,' she said, somewhat drily.

'What a practical woman you are.'

'Someone has to be. What on earth will you do with a castle?'

'Give it to you. As a wedding present.'

Before her brain could unscramble sufficiently to formulate a sensible response and instruct her mouth to pass it on, the pilot had set the helicopter down with a bump, and Fergus had jumped down and was offering her a hand.

She knew she shouldn't take it. She should stay right where she was and tell the pilot to take her straight back to Melchester.

'You don't like it. Is it a moat or nothing?' Fergus asked as she hesitated, his face mock tragic. 'I knew it. I told the estate agent it wouldn't do. May warned me you're a perfectionist—'

'Don't be silly.'

'It's quite all right,' he said. 'I understand.'

'Fergus, it's quite beautiful.'

'Beautiful?'

'I love it.' She shouldn't have said that. She shouldn't be encouraging him. 'It doesn't need a moat. I mean, there's a river, isn't there? And there's even a swan, look...'

He didn't take his eyes off her. 'Two, actually. A pair. They mate for life, did you know?'

'Everyone knows that,' she said, cross with herself but quite unable to be cross with him. 'Come on. You'd better show me around.' And she put her hands on his shoulders so that he could lift her down.

They explored the small manor house built by some Stuart gentleman with lands along the borders. It was crumbling in places with age and neglect, but it was unbelievably beautiful.

'Come and see the tower,' he said, taking her hand, holding it as they wound up the stone staircase. 'It's like something out of a fairy tale.' And he was right. At the top of the staircase was a large round chamber, sparsely furnished in Jacobean pieces, with a large four-poster bed as the centrepiece.

'However did they get it up here?' Veronica asked.

'I guess it was built up here. It would have gone long ago, but no one could figure out how to get it out. I thought we might use this room.' He crossed to the window and she followed him. 'Just look at that view.'

It was green and soft, with the Brecon Beacons rising majestically in front of them. It was perfect. He was perfect. She was the only one flawed, damaged...

She shivered, and he took her into his arms. 'Don't worry, the heating engineers are coming in next week.'

It wasn't the cold that was making her shiver... Then, as she took in what he'd just said, her head flew up from his shoulder.

'You told me you hadn't bought it!'

'You asked me to,' he replied.

For a moment she just stood there, too shaken to say anything. And then she found her voice. 'You're impossible, do you know that?' She tried to jerk away from him, but he kept her within the circle of his arms, refusing to let her go. 'You think that all you have to do is click your fingers and the whole world will jump to attention. Well, I'm here to tell you that you're wrong. I didn't ask for a castle and I don't want a castle—' Even to her own ears she was beginning to sound a little desperate.

A lazy smile emphasised the sensuality of his lower lip as he glanced at her foot, then back to her face. 'Stamping your foot again? It's getting to be a habit.'

'Did I say impossible?' she said, with dangerous calm. Then she let rip. 'I meant *infuriating*!'

'You know, you're quite adorable when you're angry, Veronica. It must be the contrast with that cool, butter-wouldn't-melt-in-your-mouth front you like to wear.'

'Are you surprised?' she demanded. 'You could enrage a sloth.'

He just laughed. 'Now you've got two bright pink spots,' he said. 'One there—' he kissed her cheek '—and another one there.' He kissed her other cheek. Then he kissed her mouth.

She knew she should resist him. She was angry with herself for having got them both into this impossible situation, but she refused to take responsibility for this latest nonsense—this was all his own doing.

'You really are the most provoking man,' she said

eventually, when he allowed her to speak. But her anger had long since evaporated in the heat of his kisses, and now had all the impact of jelly that wouldn't set.

'But you love me anyway,' he murmured, his mouth doing indescribable things to her neck.

'Did I say that?' Her voice was like cobweb. 'When did I say that?'

'You need reminding?' His hand was low on her back, his thumb gentling her vertebrae through the silk of her shirt, sending warm flickers of desire coursing through her.

'No...' she said quickly. But he reminded her anyway, and she began to whimper softly as she clung to him.

'You're sure?'

'Please...'

'Please stop or please go on?'

How could he be so controlled when she was falling apart? 'I'll give you a hundred years...'

'Then promise you'll marry me.'

The bones in her legs were dissolving. 'I thought I had.'

'No, darling, you just didn't say no when I asked you. You're counting on me changing my mind.' She jerked back, stared at him. 'I won't. Promise me,' he said, just a little roughly.

'You're serious?'

'I've never been more serious about anything in my life. The world is not a perfect place, Veronica. We can't have everything; if I can have you I shall be content.' There was something so intense, so desperate, in his eyes that she couldn't doubt it. 'Will you marry me?'

'In November...' she hedged.

'Not November. I've booked the church for the third Saturday in July.'

'July! That's impossible!'

'Nothing is impossible. You haven't been the only one who's been busy this week.'

'But my mother—'

'Leave your mother to me.'

Her heart was pounding like a copper kettledrum. 'And if I refuse?'

The lazy smile made its slow way up his face to his eyes. 'Why do you think I brought you here before I asked you? Say no and you'll stay locked up in this tower until you change your mind,' he said.

She didn't doubt him for one moment. Just as she no longer doubted the power of his love to endure whatever the future held.

She smiled very slowly. 'You've got until Monday to convince me,' she said.

'Will the godparents step forward?' the vicar asked.

The parish church was full to overflowing, and Veronica smiled down at the baby lying contentedly in her arms, finger tightly holding on to hers, dark eyes fixed on her face. She glanced up at Fergus as he leaned forward and touched the baby's head very gently, his finger teasing at the dark curls, before he looked up and for a moment their eyes met, held...

Then Veronica turned and surrendered her baby to Poppy before she, Richard and Nick stepped up to the font.

The vicar took the baby. 'Name this child,' he said.

'Charles Fergus Grant,' Poppy declared in her clear, bright voice.

'Charles Fergus Grant, I baptise thee…'

Charlie Kavanagh let out a wail of outrage as the vicar poured water over his head, and Fergus sought out and held Veronica's hand in his, squeezed it hard.

Her throat was tight with emotion. This was a day she had never dreamt of, never dared to imagine—their son Charlie was a bonus, an unexpected but joyous addition to their lives.

She knew that Fergus was watching her, but she could scarcely dare to turn and look at him, knowing that this darling man would be struggling to hold back his own tears of joy. Knowing that he loved her so much he would have given up this for her.

Neither of them was in any doubt of the miracle that had happened for them. It had started as such a very small thing, on the eight-fifteen from Melchester, but Fergus had recognised it, nurtured it with the power of his love, his faith that whatever the future held life would be good.